BARBAR

Harlequin Presents and bestselling author Charlotte Lamb welcome you to the world of Barbary Wharf.

In this fascinating saga, you'll experience all the intrigue and glamour of the international world of journalism. You'll watch the inner workings of a newsroom, share the secrets discussed behind closed doors, travel to the most thrilling cities in the world. Join the players in this high-stakes game as they gamble for the biggest prize of all—true love.

In Book One, *Besieged*, you met Nick Caspian and Gina Tyrrell, whose dramatic story of passion and heartache unfolds throughout this series. You also watched as Hazel Forbes and Piet van Leyden fell in love. In *Battle for Possession*, the love and the passion continue, but it isn't until Roz Amery and Daniel Bruneille clash that the real battle begins!

Don't miss these unforgettable romantic adventures each month in Harlequin Presents—the most popular romance fiction series in the world.

The Editors

THE SENTINEL

SIR GEORGE TYRRELL DEAD

NEWSPAPER VETERAN SUFFERS HEART ATTACK AT CITY HOTEL

LONDON—Sir George Tyrrell, whose family has owned the *Sentinel* newspaper for the past eighty years, died of a heart attack suffered during a banquet celebrating the paper's move to Barbary Wharf. The attack was preceded by a loud argument between Sir George and Mr. Philip Slade. Sources close to both men claim they were discussing Mr. Slade's sale of *Sentinel* stock to newcomer Nick Caspian.

Sir George's death leaves in its wake an ownership battle between Gina Tyrrell, the widow of Sir George's grandson, and Nick Caspian, international media tycoon. Neither Mrs. Tyrrell nor Mr. Caspian could be reached for comment regarding a possible takeover, nor to confirm or deny rumors regarding the closeness of their personal relationship.

BARBARY WHARF COMPLEX OPENS AMID *SENTINEL* TURMOIL

LONDON—After years of delay, the *Sentinel*'s Barbary Wharf offices have officially opened. The state-of-the-art dockside premises replace the paper's nineteenth century home on Fleet Street where the paper has been published for eighty years. A company spokesperson has confirmed that the sale of the Fleet Street building is still pending.

The move, beset by labor problems, accidents and financial difficulties, coincides with reports of a management reorganization at the paper. Nick Caspian, owner of several European newspaper groups, has reportedly acquired majority shares in the *Sentinel*. Sources close to Mr. Caspian claim the *Sentinel* is to be the first of many British newspapers he plans to acquire to augment his media empire. Caspian is said to have injected the much-needed capital that has allowed the Barbary Wharf complex to finally open.

Charlotte Lamb

Battle For Possession

BARBARY WHARF

Harlequin Books

TORONTO • NEW YORK • LONDON
AMSTERDAM • PARIS • SYDNEY • HAMBURG
STOCKHOLM • ATHENS • TOKYO • MILAN
MADRID • WARSAW • BUDAPEST • AUCKLAND

Harlequin Presents first edition November 1992
ISBN 0-373-11509-1

Original hardcover edition published in 1992
by Mills & Boon Limited

BATTLE FOR POSSESSION

BARBARY WHARF

For more than one hundred years, London's Fleet Street has been the heartbeat of Britain's major newspaper and magazine industries. But decaying buildings and the high cost of inner-city real estate have forced many companies to relocate dockside, down by the Thames River.

The owner of one such company, Sir George Tyrrell, had a dream, a vision of leading his newspaper, the *Sentinel,* into the twenty-first century with a huge, ultramodern complex called Barbary Wharf. But without additional money and time, the dream—and perhaps even the newspaper—will die.

Enter Nick Caspian, international media tycoon. The man with all the desire and the money to take over the *Sentinel.* Will he succeed and if he does, will he change the *Sentinel* beyond recognition? Will he change the life of Gina Tyrrell, a woman who's experienced his desires firsthand?

And what of the people behind the scenes at the *Sentinel?* Will foreign affairs correspondent Roz Amery come to terms with reporting to Daniel Bruneille, a man she finds totally intolerable? Even if Daniel is the only man who can help her locate her missing father?

BARBARY WHARF

CAST OF CHARACTERS

Gina Tyrrell—The young widow of Sir George Tyrrell's beloved grandson. Devastated by her husband's death, she devoted herself entirely to Sir George's well-being. And now she will devote herself entirely to his paper, the *Sentinel*.

Nick Caspian—International media tycoon with playboy reputation. Owns and operates newspapers all over Europe, and has now set his sights on Britain—starting with the *Sentinel*.

Hazel Forbes—Gina's loyal colleague at the *Sentinel*. Efficient and businesslike, she appeared to have no time for outside interests—until she met Piet.

Piet van Leyden—Chief architect for Nick Caspian's newspaper group, eager to take over supervision of the Barbary Wharf complex. Blond, Dutch and charming, he travels extensively around the world and is fluent in several languages.

Roz Amery—Foreign affairs correspondent. The daughter of an internationally acclaimed journalist, she is fiercely ambitious.

Daniel Bruneille—Chief foreign affairs editor. Rules the department with an iron fist. Fiery and temperamental, he is nevertheless admired and respected.

Des Amery—Roz's father. A renowned journalist who currently lives in Montreal, Canada, but spends much of his time in Paris.

Irena Olivero—A mysterious and beautiful young woman often seen in Des Amery's company in Paris.

CHAPTER ONE

Roz Amery put the phone down, frowning. It was the fifth time she had tried to ring her father without getting a reply. Where could he be?

She had begun to ring him within an hour of Sir George Tyrrell's death, knowing he would want to hear the news from her, rather than hear it on the radio or read it in a newspaper. He had thought a lot of the old man. Sir George was one of the old school of newspaper proprietors: autocratic, stubborn, but a man of deep, instinctive warmth. The two men had often disagreed, could be locked in battle for hours over some matter of editorial policy, but they had respected and liked each other, and she knew Des would want to be at the funeral. The question was, how was she going to find him in time?

Usually, if he was going away, he let her know before he went, but the last time she had spoken to him he had talked as if he would be staying put in Montreal for the foreseeable future.

'My roving days are over,' he had said, a smile in his voice. 'I've got a cat to feed and my autobiography to write—so I won't be coming to London this spring, after all.'

'Not even for a few days, Des?' she had asked, disappointed. 'I haven't seen you for months!'

'You must come here, Roz,' he had said. 'You can have my spare bedroom; you'll love it. It has a wonderful view of the river, and across the street there is one of the best restaurants in Montreal. Food as good as any I've eaten in Paris! I never need to cook a meal.'

'You lazy man!' she had teased, then said more seriously, 'I'm glad you're enjoying life back in your old home town.'

She had been afraid he would find retirement tedious, but in fact he had retired from journalism only to become a full-time writer, and he was just as busy, in a different way, and obviously loving life in the city where he had been born.

It hadn't surprised Roz when he'd chosen to retire there. He had always meant to go back one day, when he stopped wandering the earth.

The child of a mixed marriage—his mother having been French-Canadian and his father a Montreal-born Anglophone, of English descent, Desmond had grown up bilingual, able to fit into either culture. Maybe it had been that early glimpse of a divided culture that had made him a foreign correspondent, fascinated by the foreign and the complex? He had always written with sympathy and understanding of places on the earth torn apart by such divisions; that was what had made him an exceptional reporter.

Her brow corrugated, Roz looked out of the window at the wild, wind-torn spring sky. Somebody must know where Des had gone—but who? What was the name of those neighbours he had mentioned several times? A French name... beginning with a G...

Sunlight gleamed across the rolling grey waters of the Thames and turned them blue; a gull screeched past on white wings and her vivid blue eyes followed it. The view was new to her, and such a change after working in the grey canyon of Fleet Street, where roof-tops and a glimpse of sky were all you could see, that Roz felt she would never tire of looking at the river flowing past the new complex.

The editorial offices of the *Sentinel* ran throughout the whole floor with views on four sides through vast windows—her desk looked out on to Ratcliff Walk, the riverside entrance to Barbary Wharf, and on the opposite side the windows looked out on to North Street which was where you emerged from the underground car park.

At the moment, chaos reigned throughout the building, making Roz wonder if they would ever be able to work normally under these conditions. Office furniture was still being moved into some parts of the building, the electricians were everywhere, doing last-minute work on computer terminals and connections, and telephone engineers were checking phones which had just been installed.

For some weeks now they had been making up two papers, one in the old building in Fleet Street, which went on sale in the street, and one here, at Barbary Wharf, which was merely a dummy paper done just for practice to iron out any teething problems before they really began work here.

Now they had finally moved out of Fleet Street, and, as today was Saturday and tomorrow there would be no *Sentinel*, most of the staff were not at work. She looked along the serried ranks of desks with their telephones and word processors; few people sat there although in the glass-walled offices around the edges of the floor she saw various senior editorial staff at work.

This morning's paper lay on Roz's desk; she glanced down at it and saw on the folded front page a large photo of Sir George Tyrrell, whose sudden death during the dinner to commemorate the *Sentinel*'s departure from Fleet Street was the big story of the day. His obituary appeared on the usual page inside, on the court page on which the comings and goings of the royal family were recorded. Obituaries of famous men were always written in advance and kept up to date at yearly intervals, so it would have been an easy matter to find Sir George's file and revise it for print.

Folded inside the newspaper was a give-away special issue with pieces on the great move from Fleet Street to Barbary Wharf, a potted history of the *Sentinel*, an article on the Tyrrell family, another article on the history of Barbary Wharf itself, its origins and commercial rise and fall. Slotted in between the slabs of copy were photographs both old and new—of the old *Sentinel* building, alongside photos of the ultra-modern riverside complex, octagonal and to Roz's eye faintly sinister. She much preferred pictures of the old warehouses before they were demolished to make way for the new complex; sepia, fading Victorian images of masted ships docking along Barbary Wharf and bearded dockers unloading the exotic cargo.

Roz sighed. The *Sentinel* would never be the same again, now that the old man had gone. Nick Caspian was going to change it beyond all recognition, and not merely in the way it was written and printed. The new technology—the computerisation of all the departments—was going to be mirrored in the editorial attitudes of the staff. Nick would sweep away the sedate prose of the serious leader-writers, the stately attitude to international affairs which made its columns often read like extracts issued by the British Foreign Office, the deliberate and careful reporting of home affairs.

From now on the *Sentinel* was going down-market: easier to read, written in simpler language, intended to startle, to excite, rather than to reflect a measured view of the news. Bold headlines, bigger type, shorter words, more pictures—Roz knew the sort of papers Nick Caspian's international group published and she didn't need a crystal ball to see the *Sentinel*'s future under Nick's management.

Some modernisation was a good idea, in Roz's opinion, but she didn't want the paper's serious journalism to be swept away. It was a tragedy that the Tyrrell family had lost control. Sir George had gone to such lengths to see that he and Nick Caspian each had the same number of shares, so that he could keep a check on what Nick did with the paper.

She sighed heavily, staring out of the window. Now Nick would be able to do just as he liked, and there would be nobody to say no to him.

A deep voice from behind her made her jump. '*Que faîtes-vous ici?*'

She didn't need to look round to know the newcomer was the foreign news editor, Daniel Bruneille. She took her time in turning to face him, her blue eyes wary, and her nerves prickling. Since this was Saturday, he was casually dressed in a white polo-necked sweater, black trousers and a smooth black leather jacket, but his effect was far from casual.

'You're supposed to be taking the rest of the weekend off,' he said accusingly, as if suspecting her of some nefarious purpose in being at work when she didn't have to be there.

'I came in with Gina.' Roz tried to keep calm when she talked to him. It did her no good to lose her temper; it merely made him laugh and made her furious with herself.

'I thought Sir George's secretary was staying with her?'

'She made Hazel go home, said she wanted to be alone. Hazel rang me, and I went round there and found Gina on the point of coming over here, so I insisted on coming too, although she didn't want me to. I didn't think she should be left alone.'

'Where is she, then?' Daniel glanced up and down the open-plan room.

'In Sir George's office...' Roz paused and sighed, corrected herself. 'The office Sir George was going to have. She's reading his mail and making phone calls.'

'You would think she was actually his granddaughter, not just the widow of his grandson and no blood relation at all,' Daniel said with warm approval in his face. 'She did not have to stay with Sir George, after her husband died. She was left well provided for, wasn't she? She could have gone anywhere, done anything, but she stayed and looked after that old man devotedly. These days you don't often find such a strong sense of family duty.'

'She loved Sir George,' Roz said shortly, wondering, not for the first time, if Daniel found Gina attractive. Gina was, after all, his ideal woman—feminine, gentle, self-effacing. The opposite, she wryly admitted, of herself, as he frequently pointed out.

'Obviously!' shrugged Daniel. 'But, all the same, to give up five years of your life to an old man who is no relation of yours! It is amazing these days. With anyone else, one would think she did it for his money.'

'Gina doesn't give a damn about the money,' Roz said sharply. 'She stayed because the old man was all the family she had. Her own parents are dead, you know. So she clung on to him,' she said, and gave a sigh. 'Now she has nobody, and she's going to be very lonely.'

'She will marry again,' Daniel said with maddening conviction.

Crossly, Roz said, 'Is that all you think a woman wants out of life? To get married?'

Daniel gave her a glinting, wicked look. 'Most of them, yes, especially the feminine ones like Gina. And she is so beautiful, with such a charming nature ... there will be many men interested in her.'

'Thinking of volunteering yourself?'

He laughed softly. 'You think I am her type?'

He would be any woman's type, she thought, her gaze lowered to hide her blue eyes from him. Daniel was intensely sexy, burning with all that energy; who could help looking twice when he smiled that teasing, charming smile? That was why he had never married, of course. Why bother with anything permanent when women fell into his hands like ripe fruit after one glance from those gleaming jet-black eyes?

'We've never discussed you,' was all she said, coldly, though.

'Never?' He sounded incredulous.

Roz let her eyes meet his, limpid and clear as the blue Caribbean, and smiled sweetly. 'Sorry. Does that wound your ego?'

Daniel gave her a hard smile. 'Not even a bruise.'

'Because you can't believe we don't talk about you endlessly?' she mocked.

His face tightened. 'One day, Roz, one day...'

'Yes?' she invited, opening her eyes wider.

'Rien,' Daniel muttered, paused, frowning, to stare into the distance, then asked brusquely, 'When *is* the funeral?'

'Day after tomorrow,' Roz said, and her face changed as she was reminded of her anxiety. She looked down at the phone. 'I've been trying to ring my father, but I can't get a reply. I suppose you haven't talked to him lately? You don't know if he was planning to go away?'

Daniel frowned. 'No, the last time I heard from him he said he was intending to stay in Montreal for the moment.'

'That's what he told me, too. But he isn't answering his phone.'

'He could be out.'

'I've rung on and off for twenty-four hours. He wouldn't be out that long! You know what it's like in Montreal in February and March.'

'How could I forget?' he said with a deliberate shiver.

Winters in Quebec were a very different proposition from winters in this tame and cosy landscape in England. She thought with a strange sort of nostalgia about the winters in Quebec: the raw winds, the deep, white snow which masked everything and gave new shapes, new contours to the buildings, the trees, the hills. In country districts the children went to school on skis, and lakes and rivers froze, the trees took on a crystalline beauty, voices echoed from the far distance, or sometimes there was a stillness on the air.

It might be spring already here in London, but Montreal would still be suffering below-zero temperatures, the streets covered with snow and everyone travelling around on the metro, which was not only an underground railway system, but contained miles of shopping malls, restaurants, banks, theatres and cinemas.

With everything you might need conveniently to hand underground, nobody needed to go up into the open air. The citizens of Montreal could live like happy moles in their warm burrows until April came and the thaw began. Why should her father have gone far from his apartment? She knew his routine—he ate out at restaurants or if he ate at home did so sparingly, existing on cheese and fruit and French bread for days on end. He took walks most days, but only around the district where he lived; through the narrow, winding streets of old Montreal. He visited the libraries of both the French and the English universities, when he needed a particular or rare volume, or browsed happily among the excellent local bookshops.

'Have you rung the Gaspards?' asked Daniel. 'They could probably tell you.'

Roz's blue eyes opened wide, almost violet in their intensity. 'Gaspard! That was their name! I knew it began with a G. I suppose you don't know their telephone number?'

'Some reporter you are!' Daniel mocked, and she flushed angrily.

'Directory Enquiries,' she muttered. Why hadn't she thought of that before? Every time she missed something so obvious it was another point to Daniel in their endless battle; she could kick herself.

She picked up the phone and dialled, and a moment later she was writing down the telephone number of her father's neighbours. Desmond had moved into a tall, ramshackle building in Old Montreal, within a short walk of the harbour. Once the home of a wealthy merchant family, the house had been divided into apartments; Desmond's was on the second floor.

She rang the Gaspards immediately, and a woman answered in the Québecois patois, instantly familiar to Roz from years of life in Montreal as a small child.

'Madame Gaspard?' Roz asked, and explained herself in fluent French. 'I am Rosalind Amery, Monsieur Amery's daughter——'

'Ah, I have been so worried,' the other woman interrupted her eagerly. 'It is three days now and at first I did not realise he had gone, until I saw the mailman and he asked if *monsieur* was away because nobody was picking up the letters from the box, it was quite full. I did notice that Gigi was hungrier than usual...'

'Gigi?' asked Roz, bewildered.

'The cat. She often comes to us to be fed if *monsieur* is busy or out, so it did not seem odd at first. We are keeping her with us for the moment, although she can get into the apartment through her catflap on the balcony. That should have alerted me, too, the shutters always being closed, day and night, but I had not been looking up until the mailman spoke to me. But tell your father he need not worry, I am taking in his mail and I will look after Gigi. Did he forget to tell me he was going away?'

'*Madame*, I haven't heard from my father, I don't know where he is, I was ringing to ask you!' Roz said quietly, very pale now.

Daniel had straightened and was standing close enough to hear what the other woman said. Roz was so disturbed that she was barely aware of him. Madame Gaspard was talking rapidly and Roz was finding it hard to follow her patois at that speed. It was ages since she had heard it, after all.

'He is naughty,' she picked out as *madame* slowed. 'He must have forgotten to let me know he was going away. He will send a postcard any day now and explain. Don't worry, *mademoiselle*. Your father, he is a man who can take care of himself.'

Roz rang off and looked at Daniel, her blue eyes dark with anxiety. 'I suppose she's right? Nothing can have happened to him? It isn't like him just to leave, without seeing that the cat was taken care of, and the mail held at the post office. He had a routine, when he was going away, a list of jobs to be done first. He always prepared thoroughly for a trip, even at short notice.'

'He'll be OK,' Daniel said firmly. 'Des is a professional traveller; he knows what he is doing. There will be a damn good reason why he didn't tell the Gaspards he was going. He knew they would take care of his cat, she said they always did.'

'Maybe,' Roz said in an uncertain voice. 'But it isn't like him.'

'Look, I'll ring a few people,' offered Daniel. 'See if anyone else has heard from him lately, or has any idea where he is!'

'Oh, would you?' she asked gratefully.

'While I'm doing that, why don't you go and talk Gina Tyrrell into having some lunch? Take her down to the plaza—a very good French restaurant opened up there this week. I ate there the other day, the food is terrific. If I get any news of Des I'll come and find you.'

Just for once Roz didn't get the usual irritated prickle down her spine when Daniel began giving her orders and laying down the law. She didn't even argue. She just muttered, 'Thank you,' and even smiled at him.

She took the lift from Editorial to the floor above, which held the higher management offices and the boardroom. Everything here was silent; even the phones were not ringing. These rooms had been finished first, furnished and decorated expensively, immaculately, but today they were almost all empty.

Sir George's suite of offices were handsomely panelled in golden oak which gleamed luxuriously in the spring sunlight. Roz pushed open a door and found Gina, sitting behind the leather-covered desk at which the dead man had always sat in Fleet Street. Most of the office furniture was new, but Sir George's desk was an antique; his father had sat at it before him.

Roz paused in the doorway, watching Gina, more fragile-looking than ever in her black mourning, staring down at the desk, absently stroking one hand over the highly polished wood and leather as if it were alive and could feel her fingers. She was thinking about the old

man, you could see it at once. There was sadness in the
downward curve of her mouth, in her pallor and the
droop of her slender body.

'Finished yet? How about lunch?' Roz asked and Gina
looked up, startled.

'Oh, hello, Roz. Yes, I think I've more or less finished
for the moment, but I'm not very hungry. I'll skip lunch,
if you don't mind.'

'Bad idea,' Roz said, her voice firm. 'Come down and
nibble a lettuce leaf. Why don't we try the new restaurant in the plaza? Daniel says it's terrific.' She held
out the black coat Gina had worn that morning. 'Come
on!'

'Bully!' complained Gina, but she almost smiled, and
she got up and put on the coat.

Mourning doused her vitality, made her skin paler than
usual, even seemed to dull the vibrant colour of that
russet hair. Sir George's death had hit her hard, Roz
thought, frowning. Or was it more complicated than
that? Was it the circumstances surrounding the old man's
death which had distressed Gina so much? It had been
a shock, the way he died—of a heart attack, after a violent argument with Nick Caspian, at the farewell dinner
attended by the entire *Sentinel* team. It had all happened
so suddenly, out of the blue.

Nick had promised Sir George he would not buy any
more shares in the company if he was given a seat on
the board and a share in the management, but he had
broken his word during the dinner, and bought Philip
Slade's shares. That had given him at last the overall
majority he had always wanted. When he found out, Sir
George had been so angry that he had collapsed and
died. Distraught, Gina had accused Nick of killing Sir
George, and, judging by the way she looked, she was
still in a state of extreme shock.

As they walked towards the lift, Roz wished she knew what was going to happen to Gina, to them all. Now that Nick controlled the *Sentinel* their lives would change radically, but perhaps most of all Gina's. Her entire life had been centred around Sir George and the newspaper—what would she do now?

The plaza lay on the ground level of the complex, a vast, open square set under the main building, and directly above the underground car park. A colonnade surrounded it, and shops, banks, a beauty salon, a travel agent, bars and restaurants opened into it. In the centre played a fountain surrounded with seats and flower-beds. In summer it was going to be a big attraction for everyone who worked here, but at the moment it was a wind-trap, and bitterly cold.

The two girls hurried across to Pierre's, the newly opened French restaurant, with its green and gold striped awning above the entrance. Luckily, it was half empty and they were welcomed with open arms.

'Can we have a very quiet table?' she asked the head waiter, who nodded understandingly and took them across the restaurant to a corner discreetly half hidden from the rest by a vast palm in a pot and a half-wall topped with ferns.

Roz persuaded Gina to have some white wine with her austere meal—melon and orange cocktail followed by plain grilled white fish with a salad—and was relieved to see a little more colour come into her friend's face.

'Have you decided what you'll do yet?' she asked, refilling Gina's glass.

'I was thinking of going to a business college to get some training in economics and business techniques.'

Roz was surprised. 'Oh. But... what about the *Sentinel*—what are you going to do about that?'

'We've lost control, remember?' Gina's eyes flashed with bitterness. 'He talked Philip Slade into selling his shares, so he has majority control now, and with Sir George...' Her voice broke and she bit her lip, then went on, 'Now Sir George has...gone...I don't have a job any more.'

'Gina, you still own a massive number of shares. Insist on a seat on the board. He'll have to give it to you.'

'I never want to see him again!' Gina muttered. 'He killed the old man! Sir George had agreed to let him have management control, make most of the major decisions, but that wasn't enough for...' She could not even say his name. She kept coming up to it, like a horse facing a high fence, and balking at it, falling back on saying 'him'.

'Nothing is ever enough for Nick Caspian,' Roz said drily. 'He was born wanting it all, and determined to get it, by hook or by crook. You must beat him at his own game. Get what you want. You have the weapons, the shares and the sympathy of a lot of the board. They'll back you, if only because they are going to feel guilty about Sir George's death.' She gave Gina a wry grin. 'And, of course, they're all men, and they won't see you as any threat at all, a girl like you...they'll be happy to have you on the board, something decorative for them to look at while they're working; they'll patronise you and pat you on the head, but they won't expect you to know anything about running a newspaper or have anything to say when they're discussing business.'

'They'll be right. I haven't had a proper training!' said Gina.

'You've worked for the chairman for years—you've absorbed far more than you realise,' Roz assured her. 'Why not do both? Force Nick to give you a seat on the board *and* go to evening classes? The London colleges do some very good courses.'

Gina bit her lip, her face confused, unable to come to any firm decision as yet. 'Oh, I don't know. I never want to see . . . him . . . again.'

'You're going to let him get away with it?' Roz quietly asked, and Gina flushed, then went white, turning anguished green eyes on her. Roz could have bitten out her tongue. Why on earth had she said such a stupid thing? She put a hand out to the other girl. 'Sorry, sorry, Gina, I shouldn't have said that, forget I opened my big mouth . . .'

Gina whispered huskily, 'I just can't stand the idea of having to go to him, cap in hand, to ask for a seat on the board. I'd be so humiliated!'

'I understand,' Roz said, appalled by having hurt her when she was already so unhappy.

'I wish I could think of some way of making him pay for what he did to the old man, but at the moment I can't think straight. I feel numb one minute, as if I didn't feel anything, and the next it's as if I was being torn apart.'

'Shock,' Roz said crisply, pushing Gina's glass towards her. 'Drink your wine, that will make you feel better.'

Gina laughed a little wildly. 'Yes, Nanny!'

Roz smiled, relieved that Gina could still laugh. 'Sorry, was I being bossy?'

'I just bet you were!' said Daniel Bruneille, and both girls started and looked up at him as he materialised beside them. Daniel gave Gina a crooked smile which made his thin face intensely charming, and Roz watched expressionlessly. Was he starting his campaign to interest Gina already? Daniel's sloe-black eyes slid sideways to mock Roz. 'She specialises in being bossy,' he told Gina.

'She was only being bossy for my own good,' Gina assured him.

A waiter arrived, bearing a chair for Daniel, who gave Gina an enquiring look. 'May I join you?'

'Please do; we're still on our first course.'

Daniel sat down and without even consulting the menu asked the waiter to bring him the restaurant's own home-made terrine of rabbit with prunes, followed by the day's special, which was *coq au vin*. The wine waiter appeared a moment later and Daniel settled down to read the extensive wine list with the serious expression of a Frenchman contemplating life, the universe and the best wine he could afford.

Roz knew better than to try to talk to him until he had made his selection, but as soon as the wine waiter, after a lengthy discussion with him, had gone to find the wine they both felt would drink best with the *coq au vin*, Roz asked him impatiently, 'Well?'

Daniel gave a Gallic shrug, spreading his hands. 'Not a whisper. Nobody knows where he is.'

'Who?' asked Gina, and Roz explained. Gina gave her a perturbed look.

'How worrying for you! But he has often gone away suddenly, before, hasn't he? I'm sure he'll turn up again.'

'It occurred to me that he might have heard about Sir George's death before you started ringing him, and is actually on his way to London for the funeral,' Daniel said.

'Yes, could be,' Roz thought aloud, relief making her face brighten. 'Yes, that does make sense. Somebody else might have rung him and he could have rung me to say he was coming, but of course I wouldn't have been at home then.'

'He'd known Sir George for years,' reminded Daniel. 'It could have been a terrible shock, to hear he was dead.

Des might have forgotten everything else, just shot off to get here in a hurry.'

'But he isn't here yet,' Roz said. 'If he left yesterday, he should be.'

'Maybe he has checked into a hotel, and is ringing you at home,' Daniel suggested.

Her face cleared. 'Of course. He wouldn't think of coming here, I expect, he would probably go to the old Fleet Street building. He wouldn't know we had moved down here yet. After lunch, I'll go back home and see if he has left a message on my answerphone.'

But when she got home there was no message from her father, and during the night she woke suddenly having remembered what Madame Gaspard had said. Three days, she had said, it is three days now since he left!

Roz sat up and switched on her bedside lamp. Her father had vanished before Sir George died; his disappearance had nothing to do with hearing the news, all her guesswork was right off course. She looked at the clock. Half-past two. What time was it in Montreal? She couldn't work it out, she was too tired. She reached for the telephone by her bed and almost like an automaton dialled her father's number again without really expecting him to answer, which was just as well, because he didn't. There was still nobody in.

She didn't know what to do. Her father was well able to take care of himself; Daniel was right. Des had got all round the world by himself many times in the past and he wouldn't thank her for kicking up a fuss just because he went walkabout one more time. Why shouldn't he? OK, he hadn't made arrangements for his cat and the postal collection—so what?

Stop worrying, she told herself, switching off the light and lying down again. He'll turn up. He always does. It took her some time to get back to sleep, however.

At the back of her mind she was almost certain he would appear at Sir George's funeral, but he didn't. There were hundreds of other people there, many of whom Roz had never seen in her life before, and she scanned their faces, looking for Des without success.

She was shocked when Nick Caspian arrived, although, when she thought about it, it was foolish not to have realised he would put in an appearance. After all, the Press would have picked up on it if he hadn't shown up. There was gossip enough already, since so many people had been witness to the old man's death and the row with Nick which had preceded it. They had all heard what Gina said to Nick, too, her wild accusations of murder and her threat to make Nick pay.

So, when Nick was noticed there was a buzz, a quick intake of breath, and eyes flashed to Gina to see how she would react. Nick was with some other members of the *Sentinel*'s board, they surrounded him on all sides, like a bodyguard, and maybe that was what they were.

Was he making sure that nobody could get at him, with his friends and colleagues around him as a living shield? That Gina could not angrily ask him to leave or insult him again? Or perhaps it was the Press he was trying to avoid?

He was formally dressed in mourning, a dark suit, white shirt and black tie, and looked taller than ever, very forbidding. You wouldn't lightly challenge him or offer him any trouble. His skin was pale, tightly drawn over his cheekbones, his grey eyes hooded and icy; he looked grim. People moved aside to let him pass and stared but he didn't speak to anyone, just nodded here and there.

Gina's face had stiffened and turned even whiter at the first glimpse of him, her body had shivered once, but after that she just ignored him, pretending not to see him—but how long could she do that if he actually had the nerve to come to the reception afterwards? Roz wondered.

The service seemed endless. It had begun to rain and the church was full of grey light, the heavy cloying scent of some freesias in a wreath, and the splashing of rain on the windows, in the eaves. Roz found the atmosphere bleak and depressing; she had to struggle not to cry.

Afterwards, Roz and Hazel drove back to the house in the first black limousine with Gina. The rest of the mourners followed in a long train of cars. They found the housekeeper busy with last-minute preparations, her eyes red and her face blotchy with crying. She had been with Sir George for years and was deeply upset.

'Is everything OK, Daphne?' asked Gina.

The woman nodded. 'The waiters all seem to know what they're doing—I think we will manage.'

'Do you think we ordered enough food and drink?'

'For an army,' Daphne said grimly.

Gina gave Roz a helpless look. 'We've no real idea how many people will come. I had to over-cater.'

'Wiser to err on that side,' Roz told her, and she gave a wry little shrug.

'I suppose so.'

'Anything I can do?' Hazel asked.

'Just help me welcome everyone, both of you.' She gave them a quivering smile. 'You've both been wonderful. I don't know how to thank you.'

People began arriving shortly after that, and soon the ground floor of the Tyrrell house was thronged with men in black suits and black ties, and women in elegant, expensive mourning, nibbling in a desultory way at the

cold buffet laid out in the hall and sipping the wine which
was served by the waiters moving around between the
guests with loaded trays.

Daniel came with some of the other heads of department, and stopped to ask Roz if she had heard from
her father.

'No word from him at all,' she said huskily.

'He must have read about Sir George's death, unless
he is in some very remote part of the globe,' Daniel said,
frowning. 'I really thought he would be here today.'

'So did I,' she confessed, and Daniel gave her an ironic
look.

'Do you mean that for once you and I are thinking
alike? I find that hard to believe!'

'So do I,' Roz muttered, the skin tight over her fine
bones. 'And I doubt if it will happen again, so don't get
over-excited.'

'Do you think I am?' Daniel mocked, his jet-black
eyes wandering down over her slender body in the very
chic little black dress which she had bought in Paris some
years ago and rarely worn because she did not like the
way it emphasised her figure and clung from breast to
thigh. It made her feel exposed.

Her skin hot, Roz turned hurriedly away and heard
him laugh softly. Daniel had been amusing himself at
her expense, and she was furious. When would she learn
not to let him get at her?

At that instant voices faded away, people all turned
towards the door, and Roz knew at once that Nick
Caspian had come, after all. He had no scruples about
walking into the house of the man whose death he had
brought about. Nick didn't believe in ghosts.

She gave Gina a worried look, and saw her hands
trembling at her sides. Gina had had to bear so much
lately—how would she cope with this new tension?

Nick walked straight towards Gina, shoulders back, black head lifted, his slim, powerfully built body moving without haste. On the surface he seemed calm and normal, but as he came closer Roz saw a few little telltale signs in his appearance. Like Gina, he was very pale, and his face was rigidly controlled, but there was a little tic under one eye and a slight unsteadiness around his mouth. No, Nick was not as relaxed as he tried to seem, she realised.

Roz waited for Gina to hold out her hand to him and say a few polite words, as she had with every other guest, but as soon as he reached her Gina turned her back on him and walked away, leaving him standing there with everyone in the room watching him.

CHAPTER TWO

WHEN everyone else had left Gina said, 'I don't want to be alone, Roz. I'm afraid Nick might come back.'

'The way he looked, I wouldn't be surprised,' Roz agreed drily, thinking that she would not like to be in Gina's shoes if Nick Caspian did come back. She had seen pure rage in his eyes when Gina turned her back on him, and he was not one to turn the other cheek.

Gina bit her lip. 'If you haven't got a date, and you don't mind...would you stay for dinner, sleep here to-night? I'll lend you some pyjamas. We're more or less the same size.'

'I'd be glad to,' Roz said cheerfully, and so they sat in the quiet house that evening playing cards and talking, and in the silences between them Roz heard the rustle of the spring wind in the garden, the soft swishing of light rain. This was a quiet street, at night; it was not used as a through road by passing vehicles, but in the distance you could always hear the throb of London traffic.

Dinner was a light meal of food left over from the earlier buffet. Gloomily, the middle-aged housekeeper, Daphne, told them, 'We'll be eating this for days! I knew we had over-catered.'

'Never mind, it's delicious,' Roz said, looking on the positive side and delighted with the cold salmon and salad, the fresh fruit steeped in kirsch and served in a scooped-out melon. She encouraged Gina to eat, but could only persuade her to take a few mouthfuls of each course.

Did Gina inherit this house? Roz wondered, looking around the elegant dining-room. If it did become her property, she was going to find it very lonely, living here by herself. Would she keep it, or sell it?

They were drinking their coffee in the sitting-room when somebody rang the front door bell. Gina sat upright and almost spilt her coffee.

'It's him,' she whispered, very pale, and Roz gave her a shrewd, thoughtful look. She knew Gina had been dating Piet van Leyden until recently—but there was something very personal about the way she reacted to Nick Caspian. What had been going on between them?

Daphne, the housekeeper, answered the door, and Roz and Gina heard voices. Daphne speaking brusquely, then a man's voice, but too low for Roz to tell if it was Nick Caspian.

Gina relaxed, though, letting out a long sigh. 'No, it isn't,' she said, which made Roz look sharply, curiously, at her. Her hearing must be good. Or was she able to distinguish Nick Caspian's voice however softly he spoke?

There was a tap on the door and Daphne, still drawn and a little pink around the eyes, came in. 'Mr Slade would like to see you for five minutes, Mrs Tyrrell,' she said in a tight voice.

Gina's green eyes widened. 'Mr Philip Slade?'

'Yes.' Daphne knew what had precipitated Sir George's fatal heart attack and her face was angry, a small red circle in each cheek. 'Coming here,' she burst out. 'Impudence, that's what I call it. No decency. Shall I tell him to be off?'

'I wonder why he's come?' Roz thought aloud and Gina gave her a startled, uncertain look.

'To say he's sorry?'

'Bit late for that, isn't it?' Daphne muttered, glowering. 'He can't clear his conscience that easily.'

'I think you should see him,' Roz told Gina, taking no notice of the housekeeper's comments. 'After all, he probably hasn't signed over his shares to Nick Caspian yet, and you might be able to get him to change his mind. You won't even need to say much, just cry a little bit, look wistful and pleading...'

'Oh, no!' Gina said, horrified. 'Really, Roz, I couldn't—it would be so embarrassing.'

'Not even if it means Nick Caspian doesn't get full control of the *Sentinel*?'

Gina seemed speechless, her face very flushed and startled.

'Daphne, will you show Mr Slade in, please?' Roz said firmly when it became clear Gina could not bring herself to make a decision.

Daphne looked as if she might be going to argue, but Roz met her bridling gaze head on, forbiddingly, so with a cross shrug she flounced out.

She returned almost immediately with Philip Slade, whom she announced in chilly, disapproving tones.

He hesitated, looking at the two young women, obviously taken aback to find Roz there, then nervously went over to Gina.

'Mrs Tyrrell, I'm sorry to intrude at a time like this— I was very shocked by Sir George's death, I can't tell you how much I regretted...' He broke off, looked pleadingly at Gina. 'I would have come to the funeral, but I was still trying to make up my mind what to do and until I had it seemed wrong for me to see you.'

Gina raised her eyes to him at last, searching his face to see if he was sincere. He looked more like a boy than a man in his early twenties, and she couldn't help being convinced by his pallor and unhappy eyes.

'I realise you must to some extent blame me, but at least hear me out,' he begged.

Gina hesitated. She sighed. 'Well, sit down, Mr Slade.'

'Philip, please,' he said, obeying her and taking a chair close to her own.

'Can we offer you something to drink?' Roz asked him.

'Oh, no, I couldn't put you to any trouble...'

'No trouble,' Roz said, getting up and walking over to the table on which stood some decanters. 'What do we have here? Brandy? Whisky? Port?'

'A little brandy, thank you,' he said, and she poured some into a glass and came back with it.

Roz made an urgent face at Gina, behind his back, willing her to be nicer to him. It was obvious to Roz that he was having second thoughts about selling to Nick, because of his guilt over Sir George's death, and Gina ought to deepen that guilt, play on it to make him agree to sell the shares to her.

Gina gave her a wry look, shook her head slightly, which didn't surprise Roz too much. It just wasn't in Gina's nature to hide what she was really feeling, however much depended on it.

As she handed his glass to Philip Slade Roz studied him observantly. What sort of man was he?

He was obviously in his early twenties, a slim young man with a smooth boyish face and soft brown hair which fell over one eye every now and again, so that he had to push it back with a gesture rather too practised for Roz's taste. She did not go for willowy, charming young men, and this one had very bright, very light blue eyes which she thought meant he was probably vain. She had often noticed that men with eyes like that were prone to conceit. Even his mouth was on the weak side, she thought, but would Gina notice all that? Roz knew that she was more ruthless in her assessments of people than Gina ever was; Gina was too soft-hearted to think the worst of anyone.

He drank a little of his brandy, then gave Gina another of his pleading smiles, the little boy lost look which made Roz want to kick him.

'Please believe me, I had no idea what the repercussions might be if I sold those shares to Caspian,' he said. 'He tackled me at the dinner, and I knew Sir George had made a deal with him, and Caspian was taking over the *Sentinel*. What I didn't know was that my shares would give Caspian absolute control, upset some bargain they had made—and when Sir George flew into such a rage I was quite taken aback.'

He seemed sincere, his face earnest. Glancing at Gina, Roz realised that young Slade was convincing her, at least.

'If I had had any idea I would never have agreed to sell, believe me,' he insisted seriously.

'I do,' Gina said and smiled at him. Roz watched, knowing with irony that the sweetness, that gentle forgiveness, was utterly genuine, not put on just to win Philip Slade back into the Tyrrell camp. She had urged Gina to be nice to Philip Slade, to get his shares back, but that was not Gina's way at all. She couldn't act a part. Gina was really touched by what she had just heard. She believed Philip Slade's story, and Roz had to admit it sounded like the truth. The question was, however, had he signed that transfer? Did his shares now belong to Caspian International?

Philip Slade put down his brandy glass and smiled gratefully back at Gina, extending his hand. 'If I could change what had happened, I would, you know.'

'I'm sure you would,' she softly said, letting him have her pale, delicate hand. 'And I'm sure Sir George knows that now, too. I know he was very hurt by what he thought was your desertion. He always felt so close to your family—your father and grandfather were good friends of his, he trusted them, and he thought a lot of you, too, Philip. It will make all the difference to him to know you didn't realise what was at stake.'

Philip Slade looked startled and confused, as well he might. Gina was talking as if the old man was still alive.

Roz fixed her eyes on Gina, willing her to ask if the shares had been transferred yet, or if he could get out of the deal. But of course Gina had no such thought in her head. She just smiled up at Philip Slade, her green eyes misty.

He looked transfixed, a man who had seen a walking dream. Gina in her clinging black dress, her hair the colour of burnished autumn leaves, her skin transparent and clear, her pink mouth a mournful curve, was quite lovely, and Philip Slade could not take his eyes off her.

Roz bluntly asked him, herself, at last, 'Is the deal completed? Does Nick Caspian own the shares?'

Philip slowly shifted his bemused eyes from Gina's face to her. 'Sorry?' He pulled his thoughts together, frowning. 'No, I haven't actually spoken to Caspian since. He rang a couple of times, but I needed time to think.' He looked back at Gina, his face softening again. 'As I said, I didn't come to the funeral because I still hadn't decided what I ought to do, but I think I should retain my shares.'

Gina's face lit up, and she said huskily, 'You will? Oh, Philip...'

He smiled happily at the way she was gazing at him. 'I'll get my lawyer to contact Caspian and explain I've changed my mind.'

'He might try to claim you had a binding agreement,' Roz pointed out in the interests of common sense and not kidding oneself. 'You said yes, and shook hands on it. In the financial world, that can be a binding contract.'

'Not these days.' Philip shrugged nonchalantly. 'I'm sure my lawyer can make nonsense of that.'

'Let's hope you're right,' said Roz in dry tones. 'But you do realise Nick Caspian isn't going to like it.'

Philip looked a little unnerved, but said, 'He can't eat me.' He grinned boyishly at Gina, showing off. 'I'd be too tough for him!'

It was a joke and she laughed obligingly.

Philip finished his brandy and got up. 'Well, I'd better be going, I'm sorry to have called this late, but I'd been walking around, trying to think. I think better when I'm alone, and walking helps. And I had just decided when I realised I was near your house and I saw the lights on, so on impulse I rang the bell...' He gave her that little boy smile again, and Gina stood up and gave him her hand, smiling back gently.

'I'm glad you did, Philip, thank you. I shall sleep much better tonight after hearing what you just told me.'

'I'm glad,' he said, gazing at her.

It was at that instant that the doorbell went again, with a more peremptory sound this time, and Gina jumped, clutching at Philip Slade's hand.

He looked at her in surprise, and Gina whispered to him shakily. 'It's him...'

'Who?' he asked, and then they all heard Daphne's voice out in the hall.

'Mrs Tyrrell cannot see anyone tonight...' Then her voice rose an octave. 'Here, what do you think you're doing? Come back. You can't go in there...'

The door burst open and Gina went white, still clutching Philip Slade's hand as she threw a terrified look at the man framed in the doorway.

Nick Caspian's icy grey stare flashed around the room once, taking in everything: Roz sitting in her chair, Philip's empty brandy glass on a small occasional table, Gina and Philip standing in the middle of the room, their hands entwined.

'Well, well, Slade,' he said in a soft voice that sent a shiver down Gina's spine. 'I didn't expect to find you here!' His narrowed eyes moved down to stare at the two clasped hands, and Gina hurriedly freed herself.

Philip was flushed and nervous under the impact of Nick Caspian's hard gaze, but he bravely tried to face the other man out. 'Hello, Nick. I came to tell Gina that...' He was stammering badly now, with Nick watching him implacably. 'Well, having realised I had made a mistake...in saying I'd sell my shares...I...' He broke off, swallowing, gave a sideways look at Gina and was given a gentle, sympathetic smile which encouraged him enough to finish in a rush. 'I changed my mind.'

'What?' Nick exploded, and Philip visibly winced as if the question had been a bullet aimed at him.

'I...'

Gina came to his rescue. 'He isn't going to sell his shares to you,' she said in an icy voice, and Nick switched his intimidating stare to her.

'He can't back out now. He shook hands on the deal.'

'S...s...sue me,' Philip stuttered, very red.

'You can't force him to sell, if he doesn't want to,' said Gina.

'We'll see about that!' threatened Nick. 'I won't let those shares go to you without a fight. You would get control if you had them, and you know nothing about running a newspaper. You would bankrupt us all in a matter of months.'

'He isn't selling to me,' said Gina.

Nick's black brows snapped together. He looked back at Philip. 'Then what the hell are you doing with them?'

'K... keeping them,' Philip got out. 'I shall sell some other shares, to raise the money I need. I'll keep the *Sentinel* shares, and I'll stay on the board.'

Nick stood very still, staring at him with glittering, narrowed eyes. 'Now I wonder why you changed your mind?' He turned those eyes on Gina, who stood there like a snow maiden, white and frozen. 'How did you get him to change it?' Nick bit out. 'When I came in, he was holding your hand. What exactly did you promise him if he agreed not to sell?'

Gina's green eyes glittered with contempt. 'You have a mind like a sewer!'

'I understand men!' Nick said, his lip curling.

'Not decent men,' Gina bitterly said. 'I didn't promise him anything. He changed his mind because he felt guilty about Sir George. I know you don't have any scruples or conscience, but Philip does.'

'So why were you holding his hand?' drawled Nick.

'We were shaking hands because Philip was just leaving!'

'Then he had better go,' Nick said, flinging the door open and gesturing to the younger man.

'I'll stay as long as Gina wants me here,' Philip said with a defiant look.

'That's very thoughtful, Philip, but it is getting late. Mr Caspian will be leaving, too,' Gina said huskily. She gave him a quivering smile. 'Goodnight, Philip. Thank you for coming, I'm very grateful to you.'

Nick made a guttural noise deep in his throat, like a snarl.

'Well, goodnight, and…if you want me…my number is in the book…' Philip nodded to Roz, avoided meeting Nick's eyes, and somehow got himself across the room and out of the house. Nick, however, stayed, watching Gina with grim fixity.

'Please leave,' she said without looking at him. 'I meant what I said—I never want to see you or speak to you again.'

'If Philip Slade doesn't sell me his shares, you and I are jointly in control of the *Sentinel*,' Nick drily pointed out. 'Exactly how are you going to work with me without ever speaking to me?'

Gina flushed slightly, biting on her lower lip like a child, her eyes lowered while she thought about that. It was only just dawning on her what Philip Slade's change of heart meant.

'It was what Sir George wanted,' Nick murmured, irony in his face.

He might be mocking her, but it was true. Sir George had hoped and planned for this—that she might one day carry on safeguarding the *Sentinel* and making sure that Nick Caspian didn't destroy everything it had always stood for.

She swallowed and said distantly, 'I may have to sit on the board of directors, but——'

'You'll work in the office, too,' Nick said. 'You know Sir George intended you to do more than turn up for board meetings.'

Her face turned scarlet, her green eyes fierce as fire. 'You don't really think I'd work for you, the way I did for him!'

'You won't have to. I won't be there most of the time. I shall be away for the rest of this week, back for a few days, and then I shan't be back for weeks. But we can discuss your future next Monday morning. I'll see you then.' He turned towards the door, caught sight of Roz and grinned sharply at her. 'Shut your mouth, Roz. You look half-witted. Goodnight.'

She didn't have a chance to answer that; the next instant he was gone, and Gina and Roz looked dazedly at each other as the front door slammed behind him.

'The man's a human whirlwind,' Roz said.

Gina sank into the nearest chair. 'I can't work with him! Even if he isn't going to be in London all that often, I still couldn't bear it. Five minutes in the same room with him, and already I feel as if I've been put through a mangle.'

Roz considered her, frowning. 'You look it, too. Come on, Gina, let's go to bed. I'm tired, myself. I could do with a solid eight hours' sleep.'

She slept quite well, but in the morning one look at Gina made her wonder if she had slept at all. There were dark circles under her eyes and she had no colour in her face. Roz insisted on taking her out for a walk in one of London's parks; there were early crocuses under the trees, purple and white and brilliant yellow, and knots of green buds on the willows down by the lake. Spring was coming fast now; you could smell it in the air, a freshness and sweetness which made your heart lift.

They had lunch in a little bistro-type restaurant a short walk from the park gates. There was live music: a pianist playing Cole Porter and Irving Berlin tunes throughout lunch.

They clapped enthusiastically when he stopped, and he grinned and came over to talk to them, so they asked him to sit at their table to drink the coffee he had ordered. He was a student at one of London's music colleges, he told them, and earned himself much needed pocket money by playing in restaurants and bars several evenings a week, as well as at weekends.

The exercise, the food, the music and the friendliness in the bistro had put colour back into Gina's face; she was more relaxed, smiled occasionally, looked far less bleak.

'I ought to go, I have various things to see to,' Roz told Gina as they drove back to the Tyrrell house in a taxi. 'I'll pop in and do a few hours' work, but if you want me to come back, though, I'd be happy to.'

'No, I'll be fine now,' Gina said, smiling at her. 'Thanks for keeping me company last night. I'm glad you were there.'

Roz dropped her back at home, and then took the taxi on to her own flat. She had kept cheerful, for Gina's sake, but as soon as she was alone again she felt her own anxiety rise to the surface of her mind. The first thing she did was check her answerphone, but there was still no word from her father. She dialled his Montreal number. Nobody answered.

She put back the phone and stood by the window, staring out over the London streets falling below her flat. She lived in an old Edwardian house set on the side of a hill in Camden. The view was magnificent, but the house was slowly decaying. The landlord never had it painted, so the paint was flaking away, the wood rotting. Inside, the furniture was old and rickety, the wallpaper peeling away. Floorboards creaked. There were mice and beetles. The garden was a tangle of weeds. But Roz preferred it to some ultra-modern concrete box of an apartment, with all the electric gadgetry of the late twentieth century and no charm whatever.

Her mind wasn't on the flat, or the view, however. She was seething with unanswerable questions. Why didn't Des ring? Where had he vanished to? And why had he done so at such short notice, and without making any of his usual arrangements?

The phone shrilled suddenly and she leapt to it, breathless. 'Hello?'

'It's me,' said a deep, familiar voice, without identifying itself otherwise. 'Have you heard from Des?'

Her heart missed a beat. 'No, have you?'

'No,' Daniel said, and she was immediately furious with him.

'You idiot! I thought for a minute you were going to give me bad news! You nearly gave me heart failure.'

'You shouldn't jump to wild conclusions,' he said shortly.

'Why did you ring me, if you didn't have any news?' He sounded bad-tempered—what was wrong with him now?

'I thought he might be in London because I've been ringing you since yesterday without getting a reply,' he brusquely explained. 'I was wondering what on earth was going on! First Des disappears, then you do! Where the hell have you been all night?'

A little flush crept into her face. 'None of your business!'

Daniel's voice hardened. 'I hope it's nobody at the office, and especially nobody married. I don't like complications at work.'

Roz decided not to explain. She did not like the way he was talking to her. 'Goodbye,' she said, hanging up. She half expected Daniel to ring back, and was ready to do battle with him if he did, but he didn't. Ever since she was a schoolgirl, Daniel had been ordering her around, giving her advice, criticising her left, right and centre—and she resented it, especially when he tried to interfere in her personal relationships. He was only being dog-in-the-manger about her love-life, anyway, she thought, glowering. He didn't want her himself, but he apparently thought he had the right to pick her men for her!

There had been a time when she had thought she was in love with him. She had left her English boarding-school and spent a year in Paris, living with her father and going to a local school to improve her French. Daniel had been working in Paris, too, and spent all his spare time with her and her father. Roz had fallen for him like a ton of bricks. It made her heart turn over just to see him walk into a room, and she had been sure Daniel was in love, too. His black eyes had always smiled when he saw her, his voice held such warmth. Every weekend he'd come and taken her swimming, skating, to the cinema. On the weekday evenings he'd joined her and her father when neither of them was working, and they'd eaten supper at a local bar, played cards together, or chess, or just sat and talked. He'd never actually made love to her, but Roz was sure he would, any day. She was walking on air, light-headed with happiness.

One night she'd decided to make the first move, as Daniel seemed afraid to—she had put her arms around his neck and kissed him passionately. For a moment Daniel's arms had tightened around her, she had felt his mouth move hotly, and then he had pulled back and pushed her away, held her at arm's length, and ruth-lessly ended her dream by laughing at her.

'What do you think you're doing, little girl? You have a lot of growing up to do before you can play grown-up games,' he had mocked, and the memory still made her flinch and burn with humiliation.

After that night she had avoided Daniel whenever she could, while he regarded her with wry, ironic eyes which made her feel worse. Des hadn't seemed to notice, to her relief, since she had not wanted her father to know what a fool she had made of herself. A few weeks later,

Daniel had left Paris and gone to another job, and it had been several years before she met him again. Roz had changed radically during those years. She had toughened up, determined that no man was ever going to make her feel so ashamed and sick again. When she dated, she called the tune and she made the rules. She had very little time for a love-life, anyway; she was far too busy building her career, learning languages and studying international current affairs, geography, history, everything necessary to a good foreign correspondent.

The wandering years with her father had left her with a taste for that sort of life. She did not want a nine-to-five job, always the same, never changing. Roz needed the new, the unknown, the mysterious. That was what she had hoped for when she took this job on the *Sentinel* and it had been a shock to her to find Daniel was the foreign editor and her boss. What she had not expected was that he would block her career; only send her out if he had no one else, and even then take care to despatch her to safe places, in Europe. One of the men always got the dangerous jobs, the far-away places. Roz argued, Roz pleaded, but she got nowhere. Daniel was immovable once he had made up his mind.

Roz saw little of Daniel over the following few days, but when she went in to work on the next Monday morning she found him already there. From her desk she could see him in his new glass-walled office, walking restlessly up and down, talking on the phone he held in one hand while in the other he held a Reuter tape he was reading.

His black hair already stood on end and he was in shirt-sleeves, his collar open and his tie loosened. Daniel was stripping for action, as the other reporters said whenever he started undoing his shirt, flinging away his jacket.

She averted her eyes, sat down and began going through her in-tray, glancing at agency tapes, publicity hand-outs, inter-office memos—all the paper junk which flowed pointlessly around the newspaper until it was chucked into a waste-paper bin.

One of her colleagues stopped by her desk as she was studying the morning digest of currently running stories in order of importance.

'Well, Roz, how do you like it? I already don't like working here. Have you noticed how hot it is? They've got that central heating turned up much too high and the air conditioning makes my sinuses play up.'

Roz put down the sheets of printed news she had flicked through and grinned at him.

'Jimmy, you know you have to have something to complain about or you aren't happy.'

He made a face at her. 'Well, here's something to make you happy—morning conference in half an hour and I'm sure someone will be sent to Mexico City to cover this international conference.'

'Edward is out there.'

'Edward is sick. They think it's hepatitis. He turned yellow.'

Roz was appalled. 'Oh, how ghastly. His wife is always terrified when he's abroad; he picks up everything going. She wants him to switch to the home desk.'

'Shirley is the hysterical type,' Jimmy shrugged. 'Why do you think Edward is so keen to stay on the foreign side?'

Roz gave him a frown. 'You're so malicious. Poor woman, she adores Edward; she can't help worrying about him.' But her mind wasn't on Edward's wife, she was hurriedly going through the names of all the foreign reporters not abroad on a story, and wondering whom of those left Daniel would send off to Mexico City. There weren't many people available.

'Have you had all your jabs?' she asked Jimmy, who grinned knowingly at her.

'Yes, I have, so don't get too hopeful, because I know Mexico and you haven't been there yet, have you?'

'Several times!' she contradicted, and later, when the same subject came up in the conference Daniel was chairing, repeated her claim.

Daniel eyed her derisively. 'When you were a kid!'

'The last time I went there, I was seventeen!'

'Fifteen,' he said, and she would have denied it if she could, but his gleaming dark eyes made that impossible. Daniel never forgot a fact; the tiniest detail was stored away in that incredible memory.

'And that isn't long ago!' he murmured, and everyone else laughed.

'That's why I remember it so well,' said Roz, pretending to be amused, too, burning with resentment.

Daniel gave her a level, sardonic look. 'You are not going.'

'I never get to go anywhere really exciting!' she protested.

'Yes, you do, but you are not going to Mexico. Jimmy, you'll go. The flight is booked, two o'clock this afternoon, that gives you time to go home if you need to. Don't forget to collect your tickets and vouchers from Hilary. She'll tell you which hotel she booked you into, and she'll have currency.'

Jimmy nodded, getting up. He gave Roz a teasing grin. 'Better luck next time.'

She wouldn't be a sore loser in front of the other reporters. She shrugged. 'Give Edward my love, if you visit him,' she said, adding, 'And take care not to catch his hepatitis.'

Daniel glanced at the clipboard he held. 'Now, Poland. I think we must send someone. Tom, you speak Polish, don't you?'

Tom was a linguistic genius, speaking almost every European language. He nodded. 'When do I leave?'

Daniel dealt with him, and Tom left at once, too, then Daniel talked about the main foreign stories which he thought should be covered in tomorrow's edition. He had already been up to the new editor's office to sit in on the morning editorial conference between all departments, and he had been given the go-ahead on the stories he wanted to follow up.

They had permanent correspondents in the major countries, like America, India, Japan, many of the European nations, and others. Sometimes, though, they sent out a second reporter when a country had several big stories running at once. A correspondent could not be in two places at the same time. At the moment there were a number of big foreign news stories running, taking up front page space, and almost all the London-based staff had now been sent abroad on brief trips.

Apart from Roz, there were only two reporters left on the foreign side without a job to go to. Daniel told them to start on their usual daily chore of reading all the foreign newspapers and making a precis of the contents, picking out stories they felt suitable to be reprinted in the *Sentinel*.

They got up to go, and Daniel said, 'Roz, hang on a minute, will you?'

When they were alone, she said angrily, 'Why am I always the last one to go out on a job? And don't tell me I'm imagining it. I know I'm not. You've got some sort of vendetta against me. You resent me just because I'm Des's daughter, and Sir George made you give me a job on the *Sentinel*. You hate me for it, and if there's anyone else available to do a job, you send them. Just now, for instance...I can speak fluent Spanish, I spent months in Mexico with Des, you know that, and it wasn't that long ago. Why wouldn't you let me go?'

'Because I'm sending you to Montreal!' he snapped.

CHAPTER THREE

THAT Monday morning, Gina was tempted to ignore the high-handed order Nick had given her, and stay at home.

'After all,' she said to Hazel on the phone the night before, 'I have plenty of excuses. I'm surely owed a few more days off! For one thing I have a lot to do, winding up Sir George's personal affairs. I have to keep seeing his lawyers, reading documents...'

'If I can help with any of that, I'd be glad to!' Hazel said at once.

'You are an angel,' Gina said on a sigh. 'But I think you're needed at the office. Oh, I've got such a headache... and that's another excuse for me.'

'Well, don't you go in, then. I'll explain that you're too ill,' said Hazel.

'He said he was leaving London in a few days, anyway.'

'Then all you have to do is lie low until he goes.'

'Yes,' Gina said uncertainly.

But if she wasn't there, who was to stop him sacking huge numbers of *Sentinel* staff? He had begun already, before the move, when he dismissed the editor, Harry Dearden, and the managing director, Joe Mackinlay, replacing them with his own people. Others had gone, too, but Gina suspected Nick hadn't finished swinging his axe yet. There would be other redundancies and early retirements, and she knew Sir George would have expected her to fight for those jobs. He had left her a double legacy: the inheritance named in his will, the money, the shares, the houses, of a value which she had

never expected and which terrified her—and the un-
mentioned legacy: responsibility for the newspaper his
family had founded and run for generations, and the
people who worked for it.

She had loved the old man, and she knew what he
would want her to do. So she had sighed again and said
to Hazel, 'No, I'm coming to work. Sir George wouldn't
have wanted me to run away from the first battle.' Nick
wasn't having a walk-over, not if she could help it. She
would fight him every inch of the way, to save people's
jobs and stop him changing the *Sentinel* beyond recognition.

The entrance to the underground car park was in Indy
Road, but the chauffeur dropped Gina in Ratcliff Walk,
on the embankment road above the river, which was
steely grey this morning, the colour of Nick Caspian's
eyes, and just as stormy and threatening. Rain began to
fall just as she walked up the steps, through the main
entrance.

It was nearly nine o'clock and already the complex
was humming with activity, very different from how it
had been the Saturday before the funeral, when half the
staff were not at work. People hurried to and fro, like
ants in a forest, among the potted palms and giant ferns
which clustered around the lobby. Some of them recognised her and said, 'Good morning, Mrs Tyrrell,' their
faces sympathetic; one or two stopped her to say how
sorry they had been about Sir George's death and she
gently thanked them, smiled.

The directorial floor was much quieter. She walked
along the corridor hearing a discreet hush on all sides.
Hazel, neat in dark grey skirt and black sweater, sat at
her desk in the office which adjoined the one Sir George
would have had. She looked up as Gina appeared and
smiled warmly.

'How's the head this morning?'

'Still on my shoulders,' Gina said wryly, and Hazel laughed.

'Headache gone, though?'

'Yes, thanks. How are you?'

'Fine.'

'And how is Piet?' Gina asked teasingly, and Hazel blushed.

'He's fine, too. In fact, life is great at the moment, Gina, and I wish it was for you, too, and that all your troubles were over.'

'Thanks, I wish they were, too,' Gina said, glanced at the door into the other office and lowered her voice. 'Talking about troubles, is he here yet?'

'Yes, and I have orders to show you in as soon as you arrive.'

'I bet he said "send her in", not "show her in"!'

'You win your bet,' said Hazel wryly.

'Oh, well, I suppose I'd better get on with it,' Gina sighed, squaring her shoulders.

'Would some strong coffee help?' Hazel asked.

'It would, I'd love some!' Gina took an audible breath. 'Well, here goes! Wish me luck!'

'Good luck,' Hazel said obediently, then buzzed Nick Caspian and said solemnly, 'Mrs Tyrrell is here, sir.'

'Send her in!' Nick's deep voice commanded.

Gina tapped on his door and heard him say, 'Come in, Gina.' She walked into the room and let the door swing shut behind her, her green eyes hurriedly flashing across the office to the desk.

Nick sat behind it, as she had done the other day, but he invested the room with a remote authority she knew she would never have. He was wearing an elegantly styled charcoal-grey suit and red-striped shirt, his black hair brushed until it gleamed and those grey eyes hard as flint.

'Sit down,' he ordered, pointing to a chair on the other side of the desk, and she walked reluctantly across the room while he observed her every step of the way, those cold eyes roaming from her defiantly bright green eyes, over her russet hair, which she wore combed up into a French pleat, and her slender figure in a black velvet jacket and full skirt. That stare made Gina's nerves jump and made her angry all at the same time.

Nick leaned back in his chair, drumming fingertips on the desk. 'I have to fly to Rome in the morning, so we'll have to make this short. I am presuming, since you are here, that you accept that we are going to have to work together.' He paused and his grey eyes challenged her, hard and insistent.

Gina couldn't trust herself to say anything for a moment. She simply nodded.

His mouth tightened. 'Without open conflict,' he bit out. 'I don't want you to cut me dead in public again, the way you did at the funeral, or to insult me in front of other people, either. I didn't react last time because I realised you were upset and in shock, but if it happens again I will, and you may not like what happens.'

'Don't threaten me,' Gina whispered.

'Not a threat, a promise,' he snapped back. 'We have to work together and we can't do it if you won't co-operate.'

'I'm only here because I know Sir George would have wanted me to stay on and do what I could for the *Sentinel* staff,' Gina said in a firmer voice. 'I'll co-operate during working hours.'

He considered her, his fingers tapping, his mouth tight, then shrugged. 'I hope we understand each other, then. I want you to work in this office whenever I'm not in London. The new managing director, Sean Yates, will deal with the everyday running of the paper; the new editor, Fabien Arnaud, is, of course, responsible for editorial matters. All departments will function, for the moment, just as they have done until now. I shall retain Hazel Forbes in her previous job, as chairman's secretary, and you will be my eyes and ears, just as you were Sir George's, and my mouthpiece, too, if I need one. At all times you will act only under my direction, however.'

Flushed, Gina sat forward and banged a hand down on the desk. 'I won't be your puppet!'

Nick ignored her and went on crisply, 'You'll keep in daily contact with me, and you'll see to it that I have a digest of whatever is going on here—you'll draw that up and telex it to me, wherever I may be. I shall be getting other reports, financial and journalistic, but what I want from you is your personal view of what is happening on the paper.'

'I won't spy for you, either!'

'Don't be absurd! Do you think the editor thinks I'm asking him to spy when I tell him to let me have a daily report of what he puts into the paper, and what he leaves out—and why? Or which journalist is leaving, or starting work, or off sick? Of course not. He knows I have to keep in touch with all my newspapers in Europe, and reading them every day doesn't tell me how they're being run, which I need to know. I can't be everywhere, but it's essential that I make up for that in some way. I must be aware of the situation in each paper.'

'Why?' She wasn't asking simply to be irritating, she wanted to know why, when he had so many newspapers, he felt he had to keep such a close watch on all of them. Why was he so obsessed with detail? What sort of man had the breadth to build up a huge business empire yet who needed to keep a personal eye on every tiny part of it?

He regarded her with cool impatience. 'I got caught out by a strike at one of my papers, years ago. It went on for months, and it cost me a fortune in lost revenue. It was perfectly predictable, and if I'd kept my eye on the staff situation on that paper it wouldn't have happened. It taught me the value of permanent vigilance. A strike like that wouldn't catch me unawares again, because I know exactly what is happening in every paper I own.'

Gina's mouth opened on a gasp. 'You're kidding.'

He levelled a dry gaze at her. 'No.'

'But...how...when do you do all that reading?'

'My personal secretary does a digest of the digests which are faxed to me every morning. You must meet Renata—she's Swiss, from a German-speaking canton. Of course, she works at our Luxembourg headquarters, and handles my office there while I'm away, which is most of the time. Most of my mail goes to her and if it is necessary for me to read it myself she sends it to me by courier or, if it isn't confidential, faxes it on to me. When she does the digest, if she thinks I should read personally any particular fax, she puts a star next to her brief version of it, and I look up that fax and see for myself what she thinks so important. I'm something of an insomniac so I read a great deal at night.'

She stared at him, frowning. That explained a great deal about his amazing workload. From the outside, Nick Caspian looked like a man with superhuman abilities, and when you met him it was his burning energy that impressed you. So he didn't sleep well? She remembered having heard that before, but it hadn't impinged on her at the time; now it did because she knew him better.

She knew how little he ate, and that he drank sparingly, too. Sir George had joked about him once, saying he was a robot, but he wasn't, he was human, and how much longer could he go on like this, working so many hours at such a pace?

Nick's black brows curved sardonically. 'Day-dreaming?'

She went pink, looked away, suddenly realising that she had been staring at him fixedly, and he had been conscious of it. He must wonder what had been going on inside her head. 'Sorry...' she mumbled.

His voice changed, deepened, grew husky. 'Gina, this is crazy, can't we——?' he began and her heart flipped over wildly, but then the telephone shrilled and Nick swore under his breath.

He picked it up and bit out, 'I thought I said I wasn't to be disturbed?' Then he listened, frowning. 'Oh, very well, put her on.' He glanced at Gina. 'Oddly enough, this is Renata, ringing me from Luxembourg. I'm sorry, I must take it, it must be important or she wouldn't ring me, but it shouldn't take long; she doesn't waste words.'

Gina nodded. 'Shall I wait outside?' She began to get up, but he flung out a hand in a peremptory gesture.

'No, stay where you are.' He swivelled in his chair, speaking into the phone now. 'Renata?' He smiled as he spoke, and Gina stiffened in her chair, wondering about his relationship with Renata. She had a lovely name—was she lovely? Clearly, he trusted her: she must be clever. How long had she worked for him? Her imagination was hyperactive, outlining a scenario for the two of them. Were they lovers, or had they been? She knew Nick had had other women, beautiful women like Christa Nordstrom, but until now she had never imagined him with them. The pictures unrolled inside her head and made her sick with misery.

He was talking deep, rapid German. Gina gradually found she could pick up the odd word, as she remembered the German she had learnt at school. 'Yes, you're right, it is urgent,' he said after a few moments, talking in a crisp voice. 'Leave it with me. Well, I'll be in Rome tomorrow and I'll see Vincenti then. I'll come on to Luxembourg after that. Is Esteban going to be in Rome? Well, fax him and insist. Busy or not, he must be there.' He listened again and laughed. 'See you on Thursday, or Friday at the latest. Goodbye, Renata.'

He hung up and sat staring down at his desk for a moment, as if he had forgotten Gina was there, absently drumming his fingertips on the desk. He always did that when he was thinking hard, she realised, remembering how often she had seen him do it.

Then he looked up, raked a hand through his black hair, gave her a wry grimace. 'I'm sorry, where were we?'

'You want me to send you a digest of what is happening at the *Sentinel* every day,' she quietly said.

'Yes, you fax it to Luxembourg, and Renata will pass it on to me.'

'Even more boiled down,' Gina said, and he shot her a hard smile.

'She sends me the whole fax, but the gist of what you have to say goes into her daily digest. I will read your fax if I need to.'

'If your secretary thinks you need to,' she muttered.

His grey eyes glinted. 'In your case I might make it personal.'

Gina paled and stiffened. 'Please, don't!' she said icily.

He stopped smiling. 'While I'm not here, you'll use this office; while I am here you will share Hazel's office, unless you object.'

'No, of course I don't!' she interrupted.

He nodded. 'I know you two are friends; I thought it might work quite well. She has a large office, plenty of room for another desk. Now, you will keep a copy of every word you fax me. If what you want to tell me is very confidential, you will send it by courier to Luxembourg.'

'Do I still do a digest while you're here in London?'

'Yes, I think so. Continuity is useful, and your information will build up a clear picture of the way the *Sentinel* works so that I can pull out any details I need at some future date.'

What use would he put her information to? she wondered uneasily. Was she providing him with ammunition of some kind? But what? And to use against whom?

Her voice remote, she said, 'It won't take me all day to make my report to you, though, will it?'

'I want you to get it done first thing in the morning— you should soon be able to write it in an hour, at most an hour and a half. After that, when I'm not here you will have plenty to do, representing me as well as yourself. You will be on the board of directors now, remember.' He paused, then said coolly, 'I'm making you vice-chairman.'

Gina's pink lips parted on a gasp. 'Vice-chairman? But...what does that entail?'

'A great deal of work, you'll find out,' Nick said. 'For the moment, just be in this office and hold the fort until I come back.' He got up, pushed back his chair and walked round the desk, and Gina instinctively stood up, too as he stopped beside her.

She couldn't bear to be so near him. She might tell herself she hated him, but she couldn't stop her body reacting to him. Her blood ran hot, her nerves leapt wildly, simply because Nick stood next to her. She averted her eyes, fighting to get herself under control.

'Did you know Piet was seeing Hazel Forbes?' he asked, and she nodded. 'It doesn't bother you?' he drawled, and Gina risked a direct look at him.

'I'm too busy to have room in my life for a man, anyway.'

'Oh, are you?' Nick said, his eyes flashing, but then the phone rang again and he grimaced, going back to answer it, and Gina took the opportunity of sliding out of the room.

That afternoon, Roz was on a plane to Montreal, sipping mineral water while she made notes of what she had to do there. The man next to her was drinking whisky as though it was water, and she eyed him sideways with incredulity. He was going to have one hell of a hangover next day, and would probably call it jet lag. Roz had learnt that if she ate very little on a plane and drank only water she almost never suffered any ill effects, even from long flights.

She turned to stare out of the window. White clouds floated below them, as fluffy as marshmallow. When they took off, the weather had been calm and clear; a perfect spring day.

What was the weather like in her father's sky? she wondered, frowning. Why had he left his life behind and walked away? Was he bored? Did a writer's sedentary day between four walls fail to give him what he needed? Was he ill? Or had he been called away so urgently that he forgot to make his usual arrangements before leaving?

It would be easy enough to get into his apartment, the Gaspards had said when she rang them to warn them she was on her way. Des had a cleaning woman who came once a week; she had a key so that she could get in if Des was out, and the Gaspards knew her. They offered to collect the key so that Roz could use the apartment while she was in Montreal.

Officially, Daniel was sending her to do an article on Montreal's tourism for the special features department, who were putting together a pull-out section on Canada as a holiday destination. They had already managed to pull in plenty of advertising, and the articles and photos were simply there to keep the advertising apart.

A journalist had already been despatched to the English-speaking parts of Canada, but Daniel had been asked to provide a French speaker for Quebec. Local photographers would provide a wide range of photographs.

'Thanks for sending me,' she had said to Daniel after he had explained her mission, and he had shrugged.

'Even if I didn't know you would want to check up on Des, you would be the obvious choice! You know the city better than anyone else except myself.' He, after all, was also Montreal-born, of a French family who had emigrated there after the Second World War.

'I'll still owe you a favour!'

He had given her a sideways, taunting grin. 'And don't think I won't remember!'

The look in his eyes was familiar: Daniel was always coat-trailing, trying to provoke her into a defiant outburst, but today Roz was determined not to quarrel with him.

'I'm sure you will!' she had retorted. Daniel had looked at her differently, his face changing, those jet eyes suddenly brilliant. Roz had had a moment of surprised confusion, her lips had begun to burn, her heart to hammer, and panic had swamped her mind. She had swung away.

'Well, I'd better get ready to leave!'

Daniel had hardened again, his eyes full of derision, but he had calmly answered her.

'Obviously, you'll be looking for Des while you're there, but don't forget to do the job you've been sent to do.'

'I won't,' she had stiffly said. It wouldn't be a difficult job. She, like Daniel, had lived in Montreal as a child, only leaving when her mother died and her father began his restless roaming of the earth. She had never forgotten the city, and in later years had been back, with her father, many times.

He had worked there again, at one time for the French-Canadian newspaper, *La Presse*, in Montreal, for a while, which was where he had met Daniel, who was just starting out in journalism. Roz had met many of the local media people through Des; she would soon tap all the sources and write the piece Daniel needed, and she was booked in here for three days. She would have plenty of time to look around Des's apartment, talk to his Montreal friends and see if she could find a clue to his whereabouts.

She settled down to sleep, curled up with her head on the tiny pillow provided by the airline, a blanket covering her, first taking the precaution, as she always did, of altering her wristwatch to Montreal time, in the hope of fooling her body clock. That was another trick for making travel easier that Des had taught her.

When the plane landed at Mirabel Airport she hurried through the usual procedures since she had only brought a light travelling-bag, and took a taxi to the city. To her relief, the roads were clear of snow, and the weather surprisingly mild for March.

That it had been as cold as usual was obvious from the snow still lying on the flat land alongside the *autoroute* leading from the airport to the city, but snow ploughs and constant traffic had cleared these busy roads. It was a drive of some miles, and as she watched the French road signs she got her usual feeling of home-coming.

Until the death of her mother, who had been a French Canadian, Roz had spoken nothing but French. She had lived in an entirely French environment in their little apartment in Montreal, with Maman singing in French to her, reading French fairy-stories to her.

When Maman had vanished, Roz, then only six years old, had been whisked away, by her father, to England, where he had taken a job on the *Sentinel*. Des had felt, she realised later, that he had to get away from the city where they had been so happy. Montreal was too full of memories, his grief was too overpowering there. For Roz, though, the change had been almost as much of a trauma as losing her mother.

She had never been able to forget her first day at the new school. Small and pale, stricken with confusion and terror at being surrounded by this alien tongue, she had sat at a desk, crying for her mother and dazed with misery.

A black veil fell over what followed during the next few years. No doubt she had begun to make friends as soon as she learnt a little more English and in time she could speak English fluently. She had been eight years old when another trauma had hit her. Des was offered a job on the foreign desk by Sir George Tyrrell and broke the news to her that while he was abroad she would have to live in a boarding-school.

Roz had hated Sir George, blaming him for sending her father away. She didn't know that her father had only been waiting for her to be old enough to be left behind before he took up the life of a foreign correspondent, which was what he had always wanted. All she knew was that she was being sent away from her father.

'You see, Roz,' Des had said, 'I'll be moving around the world all the time, never knowing where I'll be from one minute to the next. I couldn't drag you around with me. I couldn't do my work properly if I was worrying about you all the time, and you need somewhere safe, and peaceful, to live, and a good education. That's what I've found you, a good boarding-school in the country. You'll get plenty of fresh air and exercise, and you'll have friends to play with.'

Tears had welled up in her eyes. 'Papa, I don't want you to go away—take me with you...'

'I can't, Roz,' Des had said. 'I'm sorry, but I can't. But it won't be forever, you know. We'll have the holidays together, weeks on end in the summers.'

She had cried silently, not even listening, and Des had grown impatient. 'There's no point in crying, Roz. That's the way it has to be,' he had told her at last.

That first term of school stayed in her memory as the second unhappiest time of her life.

She had been sure Des had abandoned her, left her for ever, the way her mother had. Every night she had cried into her pillow, and even her father's postcards and letters had not consoled her. It wasn't until the end of term, when she was put on a plane to Egypt and Des met her at the airport in Cairo, that she had begun to cheer up.

Every long vacation from school after that was spent with her father, wherever he might be in the world, so long as it was safe for her to join him, and it almost always had been. She had loved those holidays, the new sights and sounds, the sun and the exotic places. Her travels had made her school-friends jealous and given her the reputation of being sophisticated and worldly-wise, a reputation she cherished.

Since she had always tried to learn something of the language of the country she was visiting, those trips had also been an enormous help to her when she'd decided to aim to be a foreign correspondent, which meant, of course, learning as many languages as possible. During those summer holidays she had discovered a flair for learning languages quickly and a fascination with other countries, other ways, other people.

No experience was ever without value, Roz thought wryly. Her mother's death had taught her to bear grief and carry on; her loneliness away from her father during her school years had made her a survivor, someone who could cope with anything life threw at her.

The taxi had reached the city now and turned off the *autoroute* into narrow, crowded streets. She looked out, at once recognising where they were from a glimpse of the towers of Notre Dame. They were close to the rue de la Commune, and a few streets from the harbour and her father's apartment. She sat closer to the glass, peering out excitedly.

Five minutes later she stood on the sidewalk looking up at the ironwork balcony outside her father's second-floor apartment, half hoping that she would see the windows open, hear him call down to her. The windows, though, stayed shut. Sighing, Roz went up the steps to the entrance of the apartments, and rang the bell against the name 'Gaspard'.

Madame Gaspard, a small, spry woman with greying dark hair, greeted her warmly and insisted that she must come in for a coffee.

'You must be so tired after that long flight from London! I am sorry my husband is not here, he is visiting his brother over in Vaudreuil. Henri works at the museum there.' While she made coffee she talked too fast for Roz to like to interrupt her. 'Are you hungry?' Madame Gaspard asked. 'Would you like an omelette? I can cook an omelette for you, faster than you can blink,

and although I say it myself it will be as good as anything you ever tasted in your life before!'

She laughed at her own boasting, but shrugged. 'But,
it's true, I love to cook, and what you love you can
always do well.'

'My father always said you were a great cook,
madame!' Roz said politely. 'But I'm not hungry, really!
Madame, do you remember the last time you saw my
father? Are you sure he didn't give you any idea where
he planned to go?'

Pursing her lips, Madame Gaspard said, 'He didn't
even hint that he planned to go anywhere. We talked of
this and that, I can't remember anything much he said,
to be honest, but if he had meant to go away he would
have told me, he always did, well in advance.' Madame
Gaspard gave Roz a concerned look, her brown eyes
grave. 'I don't even know when he left, because we were
out all that day, and when we got back Gigi was sitting
on our doorstep. The minute she saw us she began
mewing for food and I said to my husband: she's
starving, has Monsieur Amery forgotten to feed her
again? Because he does, when he is wrapped up in his
work, you know. So I rang his bell, but he didn't answer,
and I couldn't hear him typing, so I fed Gigi, and thought
nothing of it, but next day she was back, and I realised
your father must have gone away. And you don't know
where he is, either? I hope nothing is wrong!'

Roz put down her coffee-cup and got up. 'Oh, I'm
sure I'll find a note in the apartment, for me, explaining. Thank you, *madame*.'

She carried her overnight bag up the stairs to her
father's apartment, above the Gaspards. He had two
small bedrooms, a decent-sized sitting-room from which
the french windows opened out on to the balcony, so

that in warm weather he could eat outside, although in winter he tended to eat in his tiny and very warm kitchen.

The place was spotless, unusually so. The woman who came in to clean must have done a good day's work since Des disappeared. When he was here, he tended to leave papers and books everywhere. Dropping her bag on the floor, Roz prowled around, looking for some clue, although she really had no idea what she was looking for. Certainly, Des had left no note. She didn't know if he had taken any clothes; there didn't seem to be any gaps in the rows of shirts and suits, trousers and jackets, hanging in the wardrobe; and if he had taken under-clothes or pyjamas Roz wouldn't be able to tell by the neat piles of clothes in the chests.

She gave up searching his flat at last, and made herself some coffee, then sat down at Des's desk with the tele-phone and the local directory, but first of all opened Des's address book which she found in the top drawer of his desk. She might as well begin to ring round his Montreal friends in the media. That way she could kill two birds with one stone: find out if any of them knew where Des was, and at the same time see what they could tell her about Montreal's tourist and entertainment attractions.

Sipping her black coffee, she glanced down at the page at which the address book had fallen open. A brown ring filled the centre of the right-hand page. Roz frowned thoughtfully. She knew what that was—the stain left by a mug of coffee which had been placed on the page, to keep the book open.

It was one of Des's bad habits, picked up over years of working at speed, writing with one hand, holding a telephone in the other, while keeping a notepad open by holding it down with a mug of coffee or a glass. She had often protested to him about it because it could ruin a book, but Des had always slipped back into the habit in the excitement of getting an important phone call which necessitated taking notes.

Quickly, she looked at the left-hand page. There were two lines of Des's handwriting on it, in French. An address in Paris, with no indication of who lived there, and no telephone number, either. Number seven, rue des Arts, with an *arrondissement* number. Paris was divided into twenty districts, or *arrondissements,* and Roz was familiar with that district of the city, and able to place the street easily. It might mean nothing. Des knew hundreds of people in Paris—this note could have been written at any time in the past.

Except that the page had fallen open immediately, as though the weight of that mug of coffee had stood there very recently, and for some time.

She decided to ring Directory Enquiries and see if she could get a telephone number to go with this address. It was improbable, since she had no subscriber's name to offer, but she was desperate enough to make the attempt.

She got nowhere, as she had really known was likely. 'If you can't give me a subscriber name I can't find it,' the operator told her impatiently.

Roz hung up and sat there frowning, wondering if it was worth trying some other way of checking out the address? She could ring someone in Paris and ask them to see if they could find out anything. She began hunting through her father's address book, and a moment later the phone began to shrill, making her nerves jump.

For a second she couldn't move, until suddenly she became convinced, in a dreamlike surrealist way, that she would hear her father on the other end of the phone. She picked it up and whispered, 'Des? Is that you?'

CHAPTER FOUR

'NON, C'EST MOI,' Daniel's deep voice said, and Roz let out a long sigh.

'Oh, *salut*!' Then, sarcastically, 'I haven't even started work yet. I only just arrived, give me a chance!'

'I rang to see if you had had news of Des,' he bit out. 'Do I gather you found him?'

'No, there's no sign of him at all, and he's been gone for days now, without a single word.' She was more worried than she cared to admit to him, but she couldn't keep the anxiety out of her voice.

Daniel asked sharply, 'Then why did you think I might be Des?'

'I don't know,' she almost wailed. 'For some crazy reason I thought it was him. I was sitting here thinking about him and then the phone rang, as if in answer.'

'You sound jet-lagged,' Daniel said. 'Better go to bed.'

'I will, soon,' she said, then told him about the address book. 'I rang Directory Enquiries but as I have no name to go with the address they couldn't help.'

'He could have written that address any time!'

'I know, but——'

'Don't tell me. Your female intuition tells you it's important?'

She sighed. 'It's stupid, isn't it? Oh, forget it, I'm probably imagining things.'

'At least you're thinking like a woman,' Daniel drawled, and her teeth clamped together in resentment.

'Don't you ever get tired of making jokes like that? Why can't you ever forget I'm a woman? What has my sex got to do with my ability to think or do my job?'

'Everything! Just as my sex colours everything I think and do,' Daniel said. 'But I'm not wasting time arguing that out with you over the transatlantic phone. Give me this address and I'll see what I can find out about the occupant.'

With difficulty Roz pushed away her irritation with him, and said stiffly, 'I thought of ringing one of Des's friends in Paris and asking if they knew whose address it was.'

'I'll ring someone. Caspian just fired our Paris correspondent and hasn't picked a replacement, by the way.'

Roz froze, her blue eyes narrowing. 'So there's a vacancy in Paris?'

'Don't get excited,' Daniel bit out. 'You're much too young for a job like that. It will go to someone much more experienced, probably someone who has lived in Paris for years. I've seen his short-list of possible candidates and you aren't on it.'

'I didn't know the job was available, did I? I haven't had a chance to apply! How long have you known about it? You must have heard days ago. Why didn't you tell me earlier?'

'So that you wouldn't waste your time thinking about it,' Daniel said curtly.

'You blocked me deliberately!' she broke out, shaking with rage.

'I did nothing of the kind. You didn't have a snowball's chance in hell of getting the job.'

She could almost see him, the cruel, sarcastic lines of his face, the mockery of those jet eyes. 'You've been trying to wreck my career ever since I arrived in London!'

she shouted furiously. 'You've always resented me, gone out of your way to get at me——'

'Go to bed,' Daniel interrupted harshly. 'You're hysterical. I'll be kind and call it jet lag, but whatever it is I won't have it chucked at me down the transatlantic line.'

The phone clicked off; he had hung up. She was shaking as she slammed down her own phone. She hated Daniel Bruneille. That job in Paris was just what she wanted and she was fully qualified; she spoke the language fluently, like a native, she understood French politics, as far as anyone could; she knew the country intimately and was of mainly French descent. She was a natural for the post of Paris correspondent.

She was sure she could have convinced Nick Caspian he should give her the job, too.

If only she didn't have Daniel's influence working against her! Why was he always trying to get her off the foreign side? Why was he so hostile? Because she was her father's daughter and Daniel had always been jealous of her? He had hero-worshipped her father as a very young man, and envied her for being Des's daughter—but would that envy and jealousy carry on for so many years?

She got ready for bed, her whole mind obsessed with Daniel. If she was honest with herself, she had been obsessed with Daniel most of her adult life: hating him, loving him, resenting him.

How did he really feel about her? She desperately wished she knew. From the moment she arrived in London he had been making life difficult for her whenever he could. She was sure he hoped to drive her away, perhaps to another newspaper? While she showered, cleaned her teeth and slipped into the striped blue and white pyjamas she had brought with her in her overnight bag, her mind was occupied with the problem of Daniel's real feelings towards her. Sometimes she was sure he hated her, other times she had a strange, dizzying feeling that...

She broke off, her head crashing with a violent headache. She must stop thinking about him, it was making her ill. She hurried into the spare bedroom which she knew her father kept for her to use on her rare visits. It was furnished in elegant simplicity: pale lemon walls and golden oak furniture with deeper yellow curtains and a woodblock flooring on which were scattered home-made rag rugs which she remembered from her childhood. Her father had made them himself during the Second World War, he had often told her, out of cut-up old clothes which he had woven into a backing of well-washed farm sacks. He had cherished them simply because he had made them, putting them into storage if he was between permanent homes.

The bed was covered by something else she recognised: an antique quilt in gentle, faded colours. That, too, had been home-made, out of old clothes, but at a much earlier date. As a child Roz had often stared dreamily at the squares and diamonds of silk and cotton which formed the pattern on the quilt, imagining the garments from which they must have come.

This rose silk could have been from a ballgown, this well-washed gingham must have been a work dress, the strips of black forming a border around the edge might have been mourning dresses, worn for long periods whenever one of the family died as they too often did in the middle of the nineteenth century, when the mortality rate was so much higher than today.

The quilt had been made by one of her father's ancestors: a great-great aunt who had lived on a farm in rural Quebec in the nineteenth century. Roz had never been allowed to have it on her bed when she was a child, and had always coveted it, as her father knew very well. Years ago, she would have slept under it delightedly, but she was older and wiser now. Before she climbed into bed, she carefully folded the quilt with loving hands and laid it on a chair. It was too precious for anything but display, and the central heating in the apartment made her bedroom very warm.

She slept deeply, exhausted by that long flight, but woke up once after a dream she did not want to remember. Daniel had been in it, and her body still shook with aroused excitement, and burnt with a heat that disturbed her. She switched on the light and sat up, refusing to think about the dream; instead she read one of her father's books for half an hour before going back to sleep, and this time if she dreamt she did not wake up.

In the morning she still had jet lag; her head ached, she had no energy. She made a string of telephone calls, set up appointments with various useful people in the city, but it was a struggle to work when she felt so lethargic; so she decided to spend an hour at the Lisa Watier Beauty Spa, which she had visited on her last visit to Montreal when she needed to get over jet lag.

She was lucky to get an appointment at such short notice, she was told by the white-coated receptionist who booked her into the salon.

'I realise that,' Roz said. 'And I'm very relieved you could fit me in—I'm trying to recover from jet lag.'

The woman smiled gently. 'You will find a session here just what you need. Would you like us to serve you a light lunch between your massage and your hair appointment?'

'Please,' Roz said, then followed the masseuse up the stairs to one of the softly lit cubicles, where she was left alone for a moment to remove her outer clothes and put on a white *peignoir*.

The soft voice and soothing manner of the masseuse soon put her into a sleepy trance as the young woman worked on her muscles and delicately smoothed into her skin oils and creams made, she was assured, from entirely natural, organic ingredients. New Age music gently murmured in the background, the sound of leaves rustling, water flowing, clear and tranquil. It did not intrude, but like the gentle hands of the masseuse it eased her headache, made her forget her anxiety about her father, and left her in a state of relaxed calm.

She ate her lunch in the small room set aside for meals on the ground floor of the Spa. Roz chose to have salad, cheese, followed by fresh fruit. It was just what she wanted and did not leave her feeling too heavy. Afterwards she had her hair shampooed and blow-dried, spent some time having new make-up put on her face, then finished with a manicure.

She left the salon feeling refreshed and totally relaxed, and able to go on working for a great many hours that afternoon and evening. She had hired a car, and visited as many tourist spots as she could cram into the time—the Musée des Beaux-Arts, the McCord Museum, so that she could write about the photographic record of Montreal life in her article, Mount Royal with its lakes and trees, and then back into the city, along the straight wide boulevards of the modern city with its skyscrapers, which, like the grid system of New York, ran right across the city with minor roads crossing them. The contrast between old and new, the glass and concrete canyons of today with the picturesque streets of Old Montreal, would surely excite any tourist, she thought, as she drove along Sainte-Catherine Street, with its wonderful shops, and Sherbrooke Street, from which one could turn into streets full of unusual and fascinating little boutiques, bars and restaurants. Tomorrow she must venture underground into the labrynthine world in which one could shop, eat, call in at a bar, go to see a film or even a play, all without going up into the open air.

She had dinner that evening with an old friend of her father's, André Christophe, a retired editor, who had been the first person she had called.

'I haven't seen Des for weeks,' he said in surprise. 'Is anything wrong, my dear?'

'He must be away on one of his trips,' she had answered casually, and heard him laugh.

'Once wanderlust is in the blood, it can't be cured. Roz, I want to hear all about your own career—how about dinner tonight, if you're free?'

He took her to his favourite restaurant which, naturally, was a French one, specialising in seafood but with a very wide menu of classic French dishes like *coq au vin* and *lapin au miel*.

'It isn't easy to choose a restaurant in this city,' André said, refilling her glass with the delicate white wine he had chosen to drink with the locally caught fish they were both eating. 'You know, there are thousands of restaurants, literally—they open and close all the time, you have to be quick to catch some of them.'

André had become bowed and heavy in his old age, his hair grey and his face criss-crossed with lines. She gathered that he found retirement dull. His wife was dead, and his daughter had married a chef and moved back to France, to Lyons, where she and her husband ran a restaurant.

'Lyons? The heart of culinary France,' said Roz with a grin, and André nodded, laughing.

'Absolutely!'

It wasn't until they reached the coffee stage that they discussed Montreal as a tourist centre, but then André really grew eloquent. Roz took out her notepad and made copious notes of his suggestions and advice.

It was midnight before she was back in Des's apartment, and she sat up for an hour transferring her notes on to the typewriter Des liked to use, in preference to a computer. She was just going to bed when the phone rang, making her start.

It was Daniel again, and the sound of his deep voice made her flush and scowl all at the same time.

'I've been trying to ring you all evening—where have you been?' he demanded.

'Out to dinner,' she retorted. 'I do have to eat, you know!'

'Alone?' He sounded as disagreeable as ever, and she made a face at the phone, glad he could not see her.

'No, I met someone.'

'Male?' Daniel's voice was like a whip.

'As it happens, yes,' she said furiously. 'I don't have to account to you for what I do in my spare time. Why have you been ringing me?'

'I got a phone call from a friend in Paris, who checked out that address for me——'

'Female?' Roz deliberately interrupted, making her tone as brusque as his had been.

He was silent for a second, then laughed. 'Tit for tat? Yes, Roz, my friend is female—Nicole Augustin; she works on the Caspian paper I worked for when I was in Paris. When you gave me that address, I realised she lived near there, so I asked her to see if she could find out anything about the occupant and she very kindly agreed.'

Roz made faces at the phone. I bet she did, she thought. Is she in love with you? She imagined her, this other woman who eagerly agreed to do Daniel a favour. Nicole Augustin: Parisian, chic, clever, stunning. Roz knew she would hate her.

Daniel was talking while she brooded over his Paris friend. 'She went round there, pretending to be doing market research, and guess what? The apartment is rented to a Desmond Amery.'

Roz stopped thinking about Nicole Augustin and said sharply, 'What?'

Daniel sounded satisfied with her surprise. 'Exactly. But listen to this...the rent is paid by Des, but for the past year a young woman of about twenty or so has been living there, alone, although from time to time she has visits from a man of Des's description.'

Roz's gasp was audible even at the other end of the line.

Daniel laughed. 'Yes, quite a shock, isn't it? She told the other tenants he was her father. Of course, none of them believed her.'

Roz couldn't think straight, her brain was whirling. 'What on earth do I do now? If it is Des and this girl is...well, whatever she is, Des has kept her existence a secret from me, he obviously doesn't want me to know about her, so...'

'So you forget you ever found out,' agreed Daniel. 'He's a secretive old buzzard. If he discovered we had been prying into his private life he could be very angry.'

'Yes,' she said, biting her lip. 'I can't believe it...Des, of all people! I know he has woman friends, from time to time, but you say this girl is only twenty? Des is old enough to be her grandfather!'

Daniel roared with laughter. 'Don't exaggerate. Her father, maybe! But hardly her grandfather!'

'He's in his sixties! Three times her age!' Roz said with distaste and dismay.

'Ah,' Daniel said drily, and she stiffened, frowning.
'What does that mean?'

'It means that you've finally found out Des is a human being, and not the paragon of all the virtues you thought he was, and the discovery hurts, doesn't it?'

Flushed and very angry, Roz said shakily, 'Which makes you very happy, obviously!'

'Only because I hope at last you're going to grow up!'

'Oh, go to hell,' Roz said and hung up, trembling with rage and shock and disbelief in the news Daniel had given her. She could not believe it—her father with a girl years younger than she was? Impossible.

The phone rang again only minutes later and she almost didn't pick it up, but it went on and on until in the end she had to answer it.

She knew who it was, and she was right. His voice hoarse with fury, Daniel shouted down the line, 'Don't you ever dare hang up on me again!'

And then, before she could shout back at him, he hung up himself with a deafening crash.

Roz crawled into bed on the point of tears. Around her the little apartment was silent; outside she heard the traffic moving through Old Montreal's narrow streets, the blare of a horn, the squeal of tyres, the sound of jazz in a cellar bar which was open half the night. This was her father's home, he spent most of the year here now. How could he possibly be keeping a girl in Paris at the same time? There had to be some other explanation. But other than confronting Des and asking him to explain there was no way of finding out—and she knew she could never confess to her father that she had searched his apartment, looking for clues, and tracked him down to Paris. As Daniel had said, Des was a private, even a secretive man. He would bitterly resent the intrusion into his life.

She left a note for her father, propped up on his type-writer, the evening she left Montreal. She carefully didn't mention what Nicole Augustin had found out, merely asked Des to ring her when he got back. He would know she had been worried by his absence—the Gaspards would tell him that, she could rely on Madame Gaspard for giving Des a full-blown description of her phone calls, her visit, her anxiety about him.

It was fortunate that she had had a good excuse for flying to Montreal, thanks to Daniel. She had already written her article; in her note she thanked her father for the use of his typewriter to type it up so that he should know she really had been there to work. She could have faxed the article to Daniel, but decided to take it back with her on the plane, since it wasn't going to be pub-lished for a month.

She might want to polish some of the paragraphs, which she felt had been written in a workmanlike rather than an eloquent style. When you were knocking out a news story in a hurry, for next day's paper, you couldn't afford the indulgence of stylish writing, you just had to get the facts right, use short, crisp words and brief, tight sentences. It was nice, for once, to have a chance to work on your style.

She arrived back in England on Friday on a rainy morning, not having slept at all during the long flight, and found Daniel waiting for her.

'What are you doing here?' Roz asked suspiciously, and he gave her a narrow-eyed look.

'You are always so charming!'

She had the grace to flush. 'Well, you should be at the office at this time of day!'

'No, I shouldn't, because it's my day off, and for some crazy reason I thought you might like a lift into town, to save you getting a taxi.'

He had put her in the wrong again; he always managed it and Roz said in a stiff voice, 'Thank you, that was very thoughtful.'

'Not at all,' Daniel said with exquisite politeness, and reached for her overnight bag, to carry it for her. For a second she almost fought to keep it, but after one straight, cool look from those jet eyes she surrendered it without a struggle.

He drove her straight to her flat, and neither of them had much to say. Daniel was silent all along the motorway into London and Roz sat beside him staring up at the sky. The rain had stopped before they left Heathrow, she watched the sky clearing, becoming a clear, rain-washed blue. It looked, she thought vaguely, as if this might be a lovely day, after all.

Lowering her lashes to hide her eyes, she glanced at Daniel, driving with his attention fixed on the road, his face in profile strikingly individual: his black brows winglike and sardonic above those black eyes, the slash of his high cheekbones pronounced, his jawline stubborn, his mouth wide and warm and disturbingly masculine. Her eyes wandered over him, that tall, thin body tensed behind the wheel, his long hands mobile, in control.

He was a formidable opponent, she admitted, and swallowed, suddenly feeling weak at the knees as he turned his head to look at her.

Hurriedly, she looked away, out of the window, at the Camden streets they were passing through.

'How did your assignment go, then?' prompted Daniel, and she huskily gave him a brief outline of what she had done in Montreal.

'I have written my piece, but I want to do some revisions before I hand it over,' she finished.

For once he was amiable about such a delay. 'No hurry, this isn't going in for ages, but you'd better hand it in on Monday so that they can slot it in with the English Canadian stuff.'

He carried her overnight bag from his car to her front door, ignoring her when she said, 'There's no need—I can carry it, you know. It doesn't weigh much.'

'So I see,' he nodded, swinging the bag from one hand. 'You travel light.'

'A change of undies, which I wash each evening,' she said. 'A change of shirt, too, clean tights, and a pair of jeans... who needs more than that?'

She unlocked her door and turned with hand outstretched for the bag. 'Well, thanks, Daniel...'

'Can't you find anywhere better than this dump?' Daniel slid past her into her flat and dropped her bag on the floor before wandering around the sitting-room looking at everything curiously, taking books from the rows of shelves beside the hearth, picking up a framed photo of Des from the mantelpiece, a carved African figure from a table.

Roz watched him uneasily. 'Look, I don't want to be inhospitable, but I'm tired and I want a bath.'

'Aren't you even going to offer me a coffee?'

She hesitated, biting her lower lip. Having him in her flat was like having explosives here: any minute she was afraid her life would blow up around her.

Daniel swung and faced her, his jet eyes like glittering black stars. 'You're such a coward, Roz, aren't you?'

She paled, her eyes filling with anger. 'You've no right to call me that! It isn't true. What on earth makes you think I'm a coward?'

'You're the worst sort of coward,' Daniel bit out, his face taut and grim. 'You're afraid of yourself, afraid to admit you're a woman, not the carbon copy of your father you've spent your life trying to become.'

She went dead white, her face rigid. Daniel watched her closely, but he didn't stop talking in that angry voice.

'At the moment you're only half alive, Roz. You've cut off an essential side of yourself, you're starving it of existence so that you can go on blinding yourself to your real self. I suppose it's because your mother died when you were very young. You only had a father, so you modelled yourself on him, and, I admit, Des is a hero figure. He was my hero, when I was young—and not just mine! He was the role model for a lot of journalists of my generation. The difference is, he wasn't my father, and I'm not female——'

'I wondered when you would get round to that!' she burst out, furious, glaring at him. 'You're telling me my sex makes it impossible for me to be a foreign correspondent, again, aren't you? You're saying——'

'No,' Daniel cut in brusquely. 'I've never said women don't make good foreign correspondents—there's plenty of evidence to the contrary, we could both reel off strings of names to prove women can do the job.'

Roz frowned, taken aback. 'You've always made it clear you didn't want me on the foreign desk!'

'I didn't want *you* on the desk!' Daniel snapped. 'I never said I didn't want a woman.'

Her dark blue eyes flinched. 'Oh.' She was cut to the quick, too hurt to know what to say.

Daniel gave a short groan. 'Roz, listen! Sir George made me give you a job, although I told him I didn't like the idea. I didn't like having you forced on me, but I could have lived with that, if I'd believed you were good at the job. Oh, you're competent. I won't deny that. You can write, you have good news sense, your languages are excellent and you can get people to talk to you. On one level I will admit you can do the job adequately enough, but you aren't an instinctive journalist. You aren't doing the job for the right reasons. I think you went into it simply to please your father. You didn't even consider anything else.'

'Because that was what I wanted to do!' she muttered, struggling to hide the pain he had inflicted on her a moment ago. 'And whatever you say, I believe I can do it, and I still want to! It's the life I want for myself.'

Daniel's dark eyes were furious. 'Living out of a suitcase, never knowing what will happen next, risking your life, or getting beaten up, or raped, maybe. Never having a real home, because no man would want a wife who was always on the other side of the world...what sort of life is that?'

'There are negative sides,' she admitted. 'But there are positive sides, too. It's a challenge. Exciting, always different every day, you don't have a chance to get bored. I want to see the world, travel, meet new people all the time.' She paused and laughed. 'I suppose I caught the bug when I was a kid, travelling around with Des, or I am a lot more like my father than you think, but anyway it's in my blood.'

'And what about love?' Daniel asked flatly.

Roz flushed, her eyes lifting to meet his and dropping away. 'I don't see why I shouldn't manage to combine love and a career, some time,' she said, pretending to laugh.

There was a silence that made ice trickle down her spine; she risked a glance at him and found him watching her, his body tensely poised as if for some violent action.

'Love? Sex, you mean?' he ground out through his teeth. 'You aren't that stupid, surely?'

Then he moved like a snake, striking for a kill. One minute she was gazing at him blankly and the next he held her, one arm round her waist, his other hand encircling her throat in what she felt to be a threat, his fingertips resting lightly on her, as if measuring the wild beat of the pulse beneath her skin.

'What the hell do you think you're doing?' she demanded shakily, trying to push him off.

'It's time somebody drew you a few diagrams,' he muttered. 'Love isn't just going to bed with someone, there's a lot more to it than that, and it involves more than two bodies, Roz.'

'I know that!' she angrily said.

'Do you? How many men have you been to bed with?' he asked harshly.

'I never counted!' she snapped, eyes flickering.

'That many?' he mocked and she knew he wasn't impressed. 'I wonder! If you're that experienced, maybe you could teach me a thing or two?'

She was oddly breathless; she swallowed, trying to get a word out, and couldn't.

'Suddenly, you look worried,' Daniel mocked her, and the arm around her waist shifted, she felt his hand softly moving up and down her spine, pressing her closer to him, stroking her hips and the small, round swell of her behind. 'My God! You feel like a woman,' he whispered, and then his head came down and his mouth burnt on her lips, hot and sweet and demanding, leaving her so weak that she had to shut her eyes and lean on him, trembling.

Daniel's arm tightened, lifted her off the floor, and she instinctively clutched at him to save herself, her arms flung round his neck, her feet swinging in mid-air. Daniel's other arm went under her legs, she floated upwards, carried in his arms, and felt him moving. He didn't take his mouth off hers; if anything the kiss was hotter, more insistent as he walked across the room to the couch.

He sank down on it, still holding her, then they were sprawled on the couch together. Roz didn't know how it happened, but she found herself underneath him, helplessly tethered by the muscled weight of his long, lean body.

Daniel lifted his head, like a diver coming up for air, his eyes half closed, his lips parted, breathing deeply. Roz heard herself breathing with the same roughness, her heart beating so hard that it hurt.

He looked at her, his black eyes glittering, holding her down among a pile of cushions, then he slowly began to undo her shirt, button by button, and Roz lay watching him, trembling. She didn't care why he was doing this, the only thing that mattered was that this was what she wanted, and always had. She was aching for Daniel to make love to her; tremors of agonising need went through her as his fingers slid inside her shirt and pushed it back, until he could see her lacy bra, the pale breast exposed above the scallop of lace. She was dry-mouthed, her body pierced by a pleasure so intense that she cried out as Daniel bent and let his mouth touch her warm breast.

Her eyes closed then, she gave up thinking altogether and merely felt, shuddering. The sensualities were like pain; the moistness of his tongue on her nipples, the swelling of her flesh, the stab of ecstasy. She undid his shirt and stroked the faint, dark hairs on his bare chest, kissed his neck, his muscled shoulders, buried her face in him.

He had unzipped her skirt by then, sliding it downwards over her slight hips, and she felt him unpeel her fine, silky slip which clung to her hot body, giving off faint electric sparks which crackled.

Daniel kicked off his trousers with a supple twist of his body; his thighs moving against her, flesh to flesh. Roz only wore her bra and panties now; she was groaning huskily, as Daniel explored her with his mouth and hands, sending wild signals along her nerves. She was burning with desire, shaking with it, but he was in no hurry, the slow, tantalising caresses went on and on while she twisted and sighed under him. Her bra slid down, her panties followed; she was naked and he arched above her, naked too, staring down at her.

'Do you want me, Roz?' he whispered.

'Yes, yes,' she groaned, waiting for him, and then suddenly he had gone, he had got up, was dressing in a tearing hurry while she lay there, stunned and bewildered, staring at him and feeling the heated desire drain out of her.

'What's wrong?' she whispered.

'Get dressed,' Daniel muttered, not looking at her.

She went red, then white. Her hands shaking, she dragged on her clothes.

'Why?' she huskily asked. 'Why did you do that to me?'

'That was sex,' Daniel said harshly. 'Desire; purely physical, an appetite, like the hunger for food. It needn't mean a thing. Satisfy it and then you can walk away and forget the whole thing.'

Roz listened, head bent, pain eating at her like an imprisoned animal gnawing its cage.

'Maybe now you'll see the difference, between that and love,' he said in that hard, cold voice, and she felt the cruelty in it, in what he had deliberately done to her. 'Sex you can get any time, anywhere. When you're abroad in some foreign city, and you feel the need for it, you can go out and buy it, like fast food; get it from a casual pick-up, if you want to take the risk of what else you might pick up too. Sex may look like the easy option and if you live your life on the wing, like a foreign correspondent, you may never get any other option. You may never have the time to get to know anyone, learn to love anyone—and that means you'll never be a whole person, Roz. You'll miss out on everything that makes life worth living.'

She couldn't speak. She was too angry, too hurt. He had made love to her with such heart-rending tenderness, forced her to admit to herself how deeply she cared about him, how fiercely she wanted him, and he had not meant any of it. He had merely been teaching her a lesson, determined to prove he was right when he said she was not cut out to be a foreign correspondent.

Daniel walked to the door without looking at her again. He paused just once, briefly, threw one glance backwards, muttered, 'Think about it! You only have one life—don't chuck it away.'

She didn't answer and he didn't wait, anyway. A moment later he had gone, closing the door quietly behind him. The tears began to crawl down her face, she was cold and hot all at the same time, humiliated and bitterly unhappy. She would never forgive him. Never.

She worked on her article all weekend. Monday was a fine spring day and she took a bus to Barbary Wharf from Camden. The river was calm, reflecting the blue of the sky; there were daffodils and hyacinths in tubs along the walkways in the complex, and some of the printers were already taking advantage of the lovely weather to sit outside on the benches in the plaza, around the fountain. The place already began to take on a lived-in look. Wryly, she thought that any day now people would start to write graffiti on the walls.

She was nervous as she entered the open-plan editorial floor, but to her relief Daniel was closeted with several of the paper's leading foreign experts. Roz caught the swift glance he threw her through the glass, but pretended to be intent on her work, unaware of him. She sat at her desk for some time, going through her mail and the overflowing contents of her in-tray, discarding most of the stuff as out of date and irrelevant anyway, then started work on revising her article.

She had just finished when she got a call from the special features editor asking when her article on Montreal would be ready, and she said it was in her computer, and she would send it down to his terminal at once, if he liked. 'Fine!' he said. She touched the necessary keys, and a moment later the copy was on its way.

Gina rang just as she was thinking of taking a break. 'How was your trip to Canada?'

'Tiring,' Roz said drily. 'How are you?'

'OK,' Gina said but her voice didn't convince. She sounded as weary and depressed as Roz felt.

'Doing anything for lunch?' Roz asked. She did not want to eat alone today.

'Hazel and I are going to eat at Pierre's, and I'm sure they'll make it a table for three, if you can come too. One o'clock?'

'See you there,' Roz promised, and rang off.

The French restaurant, Pierre's, was far more crowded now that the staff were all in the building and word of mouth had spread Pierre's reputation. There were no free tables, noticed Roz, following the head waiter over to Gina's table. She and Hazel smiled a welcome. Hazel was bright-eyed, but Roz gave Gina a concerned glance as she sat down.

They ordered aperitifs then considered the menu thoughtfully. Roz ordered *coquilles Saint-Jacques*, delicious scallops served in their shells, followed by a fan of thinly sliced duck with an orange sauce, accompanied by a delicate green salad.

'How is everything in your office?' Roz asked, thinking that Gina was as pale and lifeless as she had been when Roz left for Canada, and still had shadows like blue bruises under her eyes. Obviously she hadn't yet got over the shock of the old man's death.

Hazel and Gina exchanged looks. 'Confusion is the best description for it,' Hazel said. 'Some staff are leaving, new people arriving—there's a weird atmosphere on our floor.'

Roz nodded. 'It's the same in Editorial. Familiar faces have vanished, and there are a lot of new ones.' She glanced at Gina and bluntly said, 'You know, you don't look well—you shouldn't be at work. What you need is a few weeks off; you should get away, somewhere peaceful. What's Nick Caspian thinking of, letting you go on working when you look like nothing on earth? Hasn't the man got eyes in his head?'

Gina gave her a rueful look. 'He's away, he was in Rome and now he's in Luxembourg; heaven knows when he'll come back. And thanks for the morale boost—you've made me feel just wonderful!'

Roz made an apologetic face. 'Sorry! But you must know I'm right. You've had a bad time lately. You ought to get away from the office and all these problems.'

'I can't do that, at least not yet—Nick left me in his place.'

Roz's blue eyes opened wide. 'He did what?'

Gina laughed. 'Don't sound so incredulous!'

'Do I?' said Roz, staring at her. 'Well, I am! Amazed and incredulous. What exactly do you mean—in his place?'

'I'm vice-chairman of the board of directors of the *Sentinel*!' Gina announced this with a certain shy pride, smiling.

Roz whistled, and looked at Hazel. 'Is she pulling my leg?'

Hazel shook her head. 'No, it's all true. While Mr Caspian is away, Gina is in his office, doing his work.'

'I've only been away since last Monday—but obviously a lot has happened,' said Roz with wry amusement. 'I suppose you aren't going to tell me you got married, Hazel?'

It was a joke, nothing else, but to her startled disbelief Hazel flushed to her hairline and looked self-conscious.

'Not quite yet,' Gina said, giving Hazel a sideways look, and laughing.

Was it that serious between her and Piet? thought Roz, but before she could ask the obvious question the waiter arrived with their first courses.

It wasn't until later that Roz remembered to ask Gina, 'Did you know Nick Caspian had fired the Paris correspondent?'

Gina looked up, expression vague. 'Yes, I think that was one of the latest round of changes. He has made quite a few correspondents redundant, and he isn't always replacing them. Because of his other European newspapers he says we won't need such a big foreign desk in future; we can get much of our background material from other Caspian International papers in whatever area we're writing about.'

'Daniel Bruneille says he's replacing the Paris correspondent. Have you seen any advertisement of the job on the company noticeboards?'

Gina and Hazel exchanged looks, frowning. 'No,' they said together.

Roz nodded grimly. 'I suspected not. You know what that means? Caspian is replacing *Sentinel* staff with his own people. You can bet that he's filling this job with someone from another Caspian paper.'

'Is that what Daniel says?' Gina asked, frowning.

'No,' said Roz through her teeth. 'But then Daniel didn't tell me the job was open until a short-list had already been drawn up.'

'Sir George always insisted that any job should be advertised inside the company, before it was advertised outside,' Gina said in slow, thoughtful tones. 'I don't like the sound of this. I wonder what Nick is up to?'

'That's pretty obvious, isn't it?' said Roz belligerently. 'He's sacking *Sentinel* staff and restocking the paper with his own people from elsewhere in Europe, particularly specialists like the foreign correspondents. I wouldn't be surprised to discover that the new Paris correspondent is going to be one of his French reporters, maybe someone who is already based in Paris. That way our Mr Caspian cuts his wages bill but keeps the best of his staff, merely relocating them with other papers, although not actually moving them physically.'

Gina bit her lip. 'I see what you mean. What on earth should I do about it?'

'I don't know what you can do. In a way it is sound economics. One of the biggest economic factors in running a newspaper is the cost of employing staff—and staff are the most expendable of a company's assets. Mr Caspian is playing a familiar game—asset-stripping, in a new sense. I expect he will sell off some of the paper's real-estate assets, too, to help him recoup the vast sum he had to pay to get control.'

'But he hasn't got control—he only shares it, with me,' Gina protested, and Roz gave her a wry, compassionate look.

'Honey, I don't want to be unkind, but you're no match for him, and he knows it. On paper he may not have control, but although you share the majority holding with him you know how ruthless he is—and how set on his own way. You won't be able to stop him doing whatever he decides to do. This appointment in Paris, for instance—you can't stop him putting in one of his French reporters.'

'Yes, I can,' Gina said, her mouth obstinate and her eyes angrily brilliant. 'He put me in charge of the *Sentinel* while he's away and I own as many shares as he does. I'll appoint a new Paris correspondent without consulting him.'

Roz had not believed Gina would risk any such action, and stared at her disbelievingly. 'But . . . you don't know any of the candidates, or anything about foreign reporting! How could you possibly choose one of them?'

'I'll appoint you!' Gina said in sudden inspiration.

CHAPTER FIVE

NICK CASPIAN returned to London in the middle of the following week, bringing with him an entourage: some of his most senior international staff, it was rumoured by one of the financial journalists, who saw them all arrive on the Wednesday morning.

'They've got a fleet of limousines to ferry them about,' Gib Collingwood told a fascinated audience in the canteen at coffee break. 'They poured out of every car, men in the best suits money can buy, women in top French fashion, looking as if breaking a fingernail would be a major industrial problem. I think he brought his entire upper management with him.'

'Some sort of conference?' someone from the sports pages hazarded, and Gib laughed cynically.

'Or a triumph. Like they had in Rome, remember— a parade through the streets, the soldiers in their best uniforms, crowds throwing flowers, the captured enemy in chains and all the booty carried on gold plates. London is their latest conquest, after all.'

Jamie Nash, the sports writer, looked impressed. That sort of poetic overwriting he understood; hyperbole and symbolism were his usual weapons. He wrote about tennis in terms that made most tennis players blush uneasily.

'They aren't going to parade us, are they?' Valerie Knight, a curvaceous blonde who worked on the women's page, asked, tongue in cheek. 'I must look out my best bikini, or is it formal dress, do you think? A cocktail dress?'

'Ask Hazel,' suggested Gib mischievously, as Hazel walked past their table, and she paused to look at them enquiringly.

When Valerie repeated what Gib had said Hazel laughed and said he was wicked, but admitted that Mr Caspian had brought some of his senior management back to London with him to be given a tour round the Barbary Wharf complex, and it was possible Valerie might run into some of them back in her own corner of the editorial floor.

'What are they like, Hazel?' asked Jamie Nash, knowing she would have seen them at close quarters.

Hazel considered the question, but then just said, 'God knows. Very polite, very well-dressed, but they have eyes like screwdrivers and when they leave my office I'll count my paperclips.'

Everyone laughed, but did not look reassured. The whole staff was nervous, with so many jobs going and nobody feeling safe. Rumours and counter-rumours flew around the place all the time, and some of them proved true, so that people walked about with the expressions of those constantly looking over their shoulder to see if it was their turn next. The arrival of the Caspian International top management naturally increased the sense of paranoia.

Gib shot a look across the cream-painted canteen and hissed, 'Some of them just walked in!'

Heads swung to stare openly. The new arrivals, half a dozen men looking far too well-tailored to be journalists or printers, stood near the swing doors, gazing around them at the crowded tables, with their easy-to-clean red tops, the queue at the self-service counter, the row of food, hot and cold, displayed inside glass cabinets, the chrome-framed abstract art which hung at intervals along the walls, the curious faces which had turned to gaze back at them with the same mild resentment animals showed to those who came to watch them in their cages at a zoo.

Valerie moved her thickly lashed violet eyes from one man to another, murmuring, 'I like the very tall guy in the pale grey suit. Style, that's what he has. More than you can say for some of the men around here.'

'Money is what he has,' Gib said acidly. 'With money you can buy most things, including so-called style—and some women.'

Valerie pretended to be deaf. 'Hazel, do you know him, the very dark man, Mediterranean-looking, with a great tan, in the pale suit?'

Hazel gave him a brief look and nodded indifferently. 'Spanish. I forget his surname, but his first name is Esteban. I heard Mr Caspian talking to him this morning.'

'Esteban?' repeated Valerie. 'Mmm...I like it. What's that in English?'

'No idea,' Hazel said blankly.

'You'll have to ask him!' snapped Gib.

'I will,' Valerie assured him, getting up and sauntering over to where the dark man was standing with his hands in his jacket pockets studying one of the abstracts hanging nearby.

'He'll be married—he's over thirty, and Spanish men are usually married by then,' said Gib with a sting in his voice which made Hazel look sharply at him. 'And if he's Spanish a divorce isn't likely; they're mostly Catholics. He probably has half a dozen kids, too.'

Jamie Nash said absentmindedly, 'Maybe that wouldn't bother Val?' He wasn't really interested, he was thinking about the possibility of losing his job, and telling himself not to worry, he would get snapped up by one of the other papers. Some people might sneer at his embroidered style of writing, but he had a big following among the readers.

Gib's mouth twisted. 'It will. She has this big moral thing about not dating married men—even if they're separated from their wives and getting a divorce.'

Hazel watched him curiously. She saw the personal records of most of the *Sentinel* staff, when they applied for other posts or had an interview with first Sir George and now Nick Caspian, and she knew that Gilbey Ralph Collingwood was a married man who had separated from his wife and was waiting for a divorce. Had he asked Valerie out and been turned down? Hazel had picked up the crackle of irritation and hostility between them just now, on both sides. Whatever had happened, they did not like each other.

Yet they were both very attractive: Valerie had natural blonde hair and a figure that made men stare; Gib might work in the dull business section, but he was one of the paper's athletes, a rugger player, runner, and swimmer—a lithe man with thick dark brown hair and hazel eyes, not exactly good-looking, but his rugged features and broad shoulders made him popular with the opposite sex.

Gib was unaware of Hazel's observation. He was too busy staring across the canteen at Valerie, her warmly rounded figure looking very sexy in a tight-fitting black skirt with a broad black leather belt, and a clinging white silk blouse which was almost transparent.

'Look at her flirting with the guy! She couldn't be more obvious if she tried.'

'He seems to like it,' Hazel said, watching the tall, dark-haired man smiling down into Valerie's bright eyes.

They were in total contrast, the two of them—he was very tall, his skin olive, his black hair curly; and Valerie was just around five feet four, with straight hair the colour of corn and a peaches and cream complexion. They made a striking pair, thought Hazel appreciatively.

'Well, of course he does!' snarled Gib, turning on Hazel. 'Away from home, on his own, and a blonde like Val makes a pass—what else do you expect? He must think it's his birthday.'

'Coming back upstairs for the conference?' one of the business section people asked Gib, as a crowd of them passed the table, heading back to their office to check the latest prices from the world's markets on their high-tech screens. The business pages were increasingly popular, and in consequence that area was given more room in the paper now, with a bigger budget. That, in turn, meant very expensive equipment, state of the art technology to enable them to keep up with the lightning changes in the markets, and a well-paid, more professional staff: highly trained experts in commodities, bear and bull markets, gilt-edged stocks, unit trusts, take-overs and all the other jargon of the financial world.

Gib gave Valerie and the Spaniard a final look, his lip curling in distaste, then nodded, following his companions out of the canteen.

He had hardly gone than Valerie returned. 'Stephen,' she told the others, picking up the clipboard and Dictaphone she had left on the table.

They all stared blankly.

'Esteban,' she explained. 'It means Stephen, in Spanish.'

'Oh,' they murmured, their indifference deafening.

'Well,' she said, 'I'm off to interview Christa Nordstrom. I hope her English is as good as they say it is.'

'Isn't she Swedish?' asked someone, and Valerie nodded.

The sports writer said, 'She's been seen around a lot with our new boss, you know! Caspian. I don't know if it's serious, but better be careful not to rub her up the wrong way or she might complain to him.'

Valerie nodded. 'Don't worry, I know all about their affair. I have a pile of clippings on her, this high.' She measured with one hand, grimacing. 'Nick Caspian isn't the only big name she's dated, and I'm not sure she is still seeing him. But I'll tread warily with her—I know she can be tricky.'

Hazel followed her out of the canteen, but while Valerie took a lift down to the underground car park Hazel took another lift back up to the chairman's floor. It had been rather peaceful in the offices while Nick Caspian was away, and Gina was in charge, but now that he was back they were riding a whirlwind again and no sooner had Hazel walked into her own office than she heard angry voices next door.

'You had no right to make any appointment without consulting me!' Nick Caspian bit out, and Gina as furiously shouted back at him.

'Did you consult me when you fired our Paris correspondent, not to mention all the others you made redundant, or sacked? Did you ask me for my opinion when you appointed Caspian International people to take their places? You told me I was vice-chairman now—but what does that mean? Is it just an empty title? Don't I have any responsibility, any power to make decisions?'

'Of course you do,' Nick snapped. 'And don't shout at me, I don't like being shouted at by women!'

'I don't like being shouted at by men, but you just shouted at me!' Gina said with cold dignity. 'And don't change the subject, either. Sir George left me his shares to make sure a Tyrrell had a voice in the running of the *Sentinel* after his death. You and I each have the same number of shares—I should have the same powers as you do. You assured me I did, you made a big song and dance about leaving me in charge, but now it seems I was just supposed to sit in this office sending you detailed reports, smiling sweetly at anyone who called, but doing absolutely nothing else.'

'You were here to deal with the day-to-day routine,' Nick said. 'Staff appointments aren't your concern.'

'Why not?' she belligerently asked.

'We have a staff appointments board to deal with them,' Nick told her.

'They don't choose foreign correspondents!'

'Of course they do, a special editorial committee makes the choice—they know what they're doing, they are all highly qualified. Daniel Bruneille is one of them, and I've asked Fabien to sit in on their discussions because he worked in Paris for three years. Normally, the editor doesn't have time to sit on an appointments board, but it will help Fabien to get to know some of the senior staff better, and his advice will be invaluable to them.' He regarded her levelly. 'You aren't qualified to choose a foreign correspondent, Gina.'

'But you are, of course!' she bitterly mocked.

'I won't be making the decision—the committee will!'

'From a short-list you've drawn up!'

His strong, dark face tightened even further. 'Stop this, Gina!'

'Deny it, then. Deny you have already picked a Paris correspondent, one of your own people, someone already in Paris, on one of Caspian International's papers!'

He stared at her, his black brows together, tapping his long fingers impatiently on his desk. 'Who told you that? Roz Amery? Can't you see that she had an ulterior motive in feeding you this fairy-story? She wanted that job, and she knew she wouldn't get it going through the usual channels; she isn't experienced enough. So she worked on your sense of grievance to get you to appoint her off your own bat. Well, it won't work. You had no authority to appoint her. The job will go to whoever the foreign desk appointments committee picks.'

'Roz didn't ask me to appoint her. It was entirely my own idea. And the Paris job isn't the only one you've railroaded past me, is it? You aren't consulting me at all about any of these radical changes you've been making since Sir George died. You've rushed them through without a word to me. I sat in on the editorial conference two days ago and I only knew half the faces. The others were all new people, and I soon realised a lot of them came from Caspian International. You're sacking Tyrrell people and replacing them with your own staff.'

He didn't deny it. 'I like to work with people I know and trust—is that surprising?'

'No, Sir George predicted it, but I was stupid enough to believe you had some decent instincts. Now I see I was wrong, but don't think you've won hands down, because from now on I insist on knowing exactly what is going on in this company. If you won't co-operate, I'll call a board meeting and we'll see if the board approves of what you've been doing.'

Nick's mouth twisted ironically. 'Do you really expect those men to take much notice of a girl without any experience of business, who doesn't know what she's talking about, and couldn't cope on her own, if I wasn't here to run the company?'

'Oh, I've no doubt some of those men will just smile condescendingly, pat me on the head and tell me to run along and play—but some of the others will take notice, especially Philip Slade.'

Nick's eyes narrowed, hard as stone.

Gina met his cold stare with a defiant toss of the head. 'You know he will. He'll vote with me, and that gives me a majority on the board. I can't lose.'

Nick's mouth was a rigid line, white with rage. He stared at her fixedly, gripping the edge of his desk.

Gina stayed outwardly calm, her chin lifted, her face unmoving, but inwardly she was all nerves and was grateful that her hands didn't actually tremble visibly. Nick was always formidable, but when he looked like that he was terrifying.

'Roz Amery isn't a suitable candidate for this job,' Nick said harshly. 'But since you feel you want to be involved in the choice I suggest you sit on the appointments committee. I won't be there. You can see how the system operates and judge for yourself who is the best candidate.'

'I want Roz on the short-list,' Gina insisted.

Nick's eyes were deadly, but after a grim pause he inclined his head. 'Very well. But when you see the others I'm sure you'll have to accept that she is not yet ready for such an important posting. Now, if that's all, I have a very important lunch date...'

'Just one more thing,' Gina said quickly. 'I don't want you victimising Roz because you suspect her of influencing me!'

'I didn't intend to,' Nick snapped. 'I know you've been friends since you were both eight years old! I realise the two of you are bound to discuss company affairs, but in future try not to talk about confidential matters, Gina.' His voice held menace and she angrily protested.

'I'm never indiscreet!'

Nick's eyes coldly doubted that, but he merely said, 'Just remember what I said, and, while we're talking about victimisation—please don't show hostility to any of my people. Whatever you think, I've appointed them on merit. I put Fabien Arnaud in here because he's quite simply the best editor I've ever worked with, and a strong European, which is what I think the *Sentinel* needs as we move into a more united Europe. Fabien has worked all over Europe, and speaks a number of languages. He's ultra-sophisticated, very clever, and he's a nice guy. Don't cold-shoulder him just because you hate me.'

'I'm not that childish!' snapped Gina.

Nick's black brows swooped upwards sardonically. 'Sometimes you are, Gina—I don't think you know yourself at all. You married too young, and your husband died too soon, leaving you living alone with an old man who treated you as a child. I suspect you got trapped in a time-warp and at heart you're still an adolescent.'

Scalding colour washed up to her hairline. Her green eyes flashed angrily at him. 'You've no right to say that to me! Do you think I don't know why you keep insisting that I don't understand business, or selling newspapers?'

'Because it's true,' Nick said tersely.

'It isn't. I've been working in this office for Sir George for five years. Oh, not as long as you've been working in newspapers, I know, but I still picked up a lot more than you want to admit. It would be so much simpler for you if I didn't exist, wouldn't it? If you could take over the *Sentinel* without having any arguments or problems. But you can't, because you don't have a majority share, so stop insulting me and trying to side-step me on any important matter you think I might block. Keep me informed of everything you're doing, or else...'

She paused and Nick bit out, 'Or else what?'

'Or else I'll have to see if I can't persuade Philip Slade to sell me those shares,' she threatened, her face stubborn.

'He won't do that,' Nick said calmly, getting to his feet. 'Sorry to spike your wonderful plan, but he's having too much fun being wooed by both sides.'

Gina gave him a mocking little smile. 'Don't be too sure.' She got up, too, as if to leave but stayed poised, waiting to see what reaction she would get, watching him through her lashes.

Nick's face had hardened, his grey eyes like chips of steel between his hooded lids. 'What does that mean?' he very quietly asked.

She shrugged, still looking down, her lashes against her flushed cheeks, and felt him staring, almost heard the whirring of his shrewd, quick mind as it worked out the puzzle.

'He's doing some wooing of his own?' guessed Nick, his voice like the crack of a whip. 'My God! And you're encouraging him, just to persuade him to let you have his *Sentinel* shares? Are all women totally without scruples?'

Gina's mouth opened in disbelief. 'You talk to me about having scruples! How about hypocrisy? That's your strong point. And, anyway, I haven't done anything to be ashamed of!'

'You don't give a fig for Philip Slade,' Nick snarled. 'You're just using him. And if he lets you have his shares? Will you go on seeing him? How far would you go, Gina, to get your hands on those shares? Marriage?'

She was so hurt and furious that her temper ran away with her. 'Why not? After all, I was ready to marry you. If you hadn't betrayed Sir George and caused his heart attack!'

Nick was very still, his breathing audible in the silent room, and she became frightened and stopped talking, made a dash for the door like a scared child, but Nick moved faster, got there first, his hand slamming against it and holding the door shut.

Gina froze, not daring to meet his eyes, trembling and breathing very fast.

'You're a liar,' Nick whispered hoarsely. 'You and me...that had nothing to do with the *Sentinel*. That was real. Do you want me to prove it?'

She had lost her courage now; she was afraid of his anger, shaking her head, staring down at the floor. She could see his feet, his highly polished black shoes, a wraith of his face reflected in them. He was watching her like a hawk watching a dove in panic which fluttered and darted from side to side but was too terrified to know how to escape. Gina sensed that at any moment Nick would swoop and take her, rend her, destroy her, and she was too paralysed with fear to be able to get away.

'I want to prove it,' Nick thickly said, his free hand shooting out to grasp her neck.

She couldn't move, she could scarcely breathe. His thumb pressed into her throat, under her chin, and her lips parted, gasping for air. She shot him one look; his mouth was inches away and she knew he was going to kiss her. He was staring at her parted lips and his eyes smouldered like hot coals. Gina knew that if she let it happen, if Nick kissed her, something terrible would happen to her. She would lose her integrity, lose her own self-respect. It mattered. Really mattered. Because if you didn't respect yourself, you were less than nothing. Her mind was dissolving, she was shaking so hard that her legs almost gave way, but she must not let him do this to her.

She fought to keep hold of the one thing that mattered—the old man, who had loved her, and whom she had loved. She owed him her loyalty, and her duty to him meant a rejection of everything Nick Caspian stood for because Nick had cheated and betrayed the old man, broken a solemn promise to him, just to win his battle for possession of the *Sentinel*. Nick was ruthless in pursuit of what he wanted, and he usually won—but he wasn't going to win his battle for possession of her.

From some inner core, she pulled out every last ounce of her courage and jerked back her head, meeting his stare head-on. Nick was darkly flushed, his face dazed, as if he were drunk.

'I have to work with you,' she quietly said, 'to make sure there is still a Tyrrell on the board of the *Sentinel*, but I haven't forgotten or forgiven what you did to Sir George, and I never shall!'

Nick didn't move for a moment, his breathing very audible to her, but then he let go of her and stood back from the door, and Gina walked out of his office with her head held high, hoping she looked a lot calmer than she felt. She heard the door slam shut and only then did her tense muscles slacken.

Hazel was at her desk, watching her with anxious sympathy. Gina staggered to a chair and sank down on it.

'You aren't going to faint?' Hazel was on her feet and rushing for water, bringing it to her in a tumbler kept in the drinks cupboard for important visitors.

She put the glass to Gina's mouth, and they both heard it chink against Gina's teeth as she swallowed some water.

Gina tried to smile. 'Thanks. I don't know what's the matter with me.'

Hazel gave her a wry, ironic look. 'I do.'

Gina avoided her eyes, took the glass from Hazel and drank some more water, trying to stop her hand shaking.

'Roz is right—you look terrible!' Hazel said, watching her pale face and shadowed green eyes. 'You really ought to take some time off, get away. A change of scene can help a lot when you're under a strain.'

Gina nodded. 'Maybe I will, later, but at the moment I have too much to do. I shall be sitting on this appointments board for the Paris job.' She gave Hazel a faint smile. 'You were right—he refused point-blank to let Roz have the job; he said it had to go through the usual procedure.'

'I won't say I told you so!'

'You've no need to! Anyway, I won a couple of concessions. I'm going to be on the committee which picks the new correspondent.'

'That doesn't meet for a week,' Hazel told her. 'You could take a few days off.'

'Really? Well, I'll think about it, then—I might spend the weekend in the country, but I must be back in time for these interviews.' She grimaced. 'Although God knows I don't have a clue what questions to ask the candidates.'

'Easy,' shrugged Hazel. 'They'll have sent in an application form, giving their qualifications and background; in fact I've got them on file somewhere, I'll be handing copies out before the meeting—read them all in advance, and you'll get some idea what questions to ask.'

Gina beamed at her. 'You're brilliant!'

Hazel laughed. 'I've always known I was, but thanks for noticing at last!' She began to make coffee for them both. 'Pity about Roz, though. I think she'd make a great Paris correspondent.'

'Well, that was the other concession!' Gina said, accepting her mug of coffee and closing both her cold, trembling hands around the warmth of it with a long sigh. 'Roz is on the short-list now, anyway. That's something.'

'It's marvellous!' Hazel emphasised. 'I'm sure she'll be very grateful to you, just for that. At least she isn't being passed over without so much as an interview.' She went over to her filing-cabinets and began to click through the top drawer with her long, clear-varnished nails. 'Ah, here they are!' She pulled out some folders and brought them over to Gina. 'These are the others on the short-list.'

'All men, I suppose?' Gina said bitterly.

Hazel frowned. 'No, I believe there was one woman.' She sorted through the folders and paused to read the neat white label on the front of one of them. 'Yes, here it is—Nicole Augustin. And I wouldn't be surprised if she got it, because she's French, already lives in Paris, and works for——'

'Caspian International!' interrupted Gina flatly, and Hazel gave her a dry look, nodding, putting the folders into her hand. Gina gave a long sigh. 'Poor Roz. She hasn't got a chance, has she?'

The phone rang and Hazel moved back to her desk quickly to pick it up. 'Mr Caspian's office,' she smoothly said, and then her face lit up. 'Piet! Where are you?' She listened, smiling rather wistfully. 'Have you seen your family since you got back to Holland?' Another pause, then she said, 'I'm looking forward to meeting them, too. I hope they will like me.'

Gina bent her head over the files Hazel had given her to read, trying not to listen to what the other girl was saying.

Piet's work in London was finished now. Nick had sent him to Holland to look at a site where Caspian International planned to develop a vast printing works in the future, near Utrecht, just half an hour's drive from Amsterdam. It occurred to Gina for the first time that Hazel and Piet would often be separated, since Piet constantly travelled around the world, like Nick. Like Nick, she thought, with a queer little pang. If she and Nick had got married that would be worrying her now, making her unhappy, those frequent partings.

'How much longer do you think you'll be in Holland?' asked Hazel and then gave a barely audible sigh. 'I see. Of course I understand, it's your job, and I'm very busy too, over here.' Another pause, then her voice grew huskier. 'Darling, of course I do...'

Gina got up and walked to the other side of the room to put the files down on top of the cabinet from which Hazel had taken them.

'I miss you too...' Hazel was saying softly, her back to Gina. 'Oh, yes, Piet, I'd love to. Next weekend? Yes, I could. I'll let you know. You'll be ringing in to report, tomorrow? I'll tell you then.' After another short silence, she said, 'Yes, he's here. I'll put you through to him now.'

She leaned over to press the inter-office key down and said, 'Mr van Leyden on the phone, Mr Caspian.'

Nick's voice grated, 'Put him through.'

Hazel obeyed and replaced her phone. Gina shot her a glance; she was very pink, her eyes bright, she looked excited and as she met Gina's eyes she smiled.

'I'm going over to Holland this weekend to see Piet, and meet his family!'

Gina beamed. 'Taking you home to meet his mother? Hazel! This is getting very serious.' She was very glad

Hazel was so happy, but she couldn't help envying her. If only...

She broke off, refusing to complete the thought. There was no point in wishing her own love-affair had not been wrecked on the rocks of Nick Caspian's ambition. Nick was a very different man from Piet van Leyden. Hazel was lucky to have fallen in love with someone she could trust her life to—Gina had not been so fortunate.

CHAPTER SIX

THE following day, the weather was so fine that Gina and Roz decided not to waste their lunch-break eating indoors. Instead, they bought sandwiches and fruit from the café-bar in the plaza, which sold a vast range of take-away food, from Indian samosas, triangles of deep-fried pastry which held meat or vegetables, to Arab couscous, and even soups in waxed cups with lids to keep the contents hot.

The Torelli family ran it; they had another bar close to London Bridge station, which Grandpa Torelli had opened just after the Second World War, and they had collectively decided to start empire-building when Barbary Wharf opened and offered them the opportunity to expand. It was still a family business, though, and today it was old Mrs Torelli behind the counter.

She was nearly seventy, but still spry and quick-witted. When one of the office messengers being served before Gina and Roz gave her too little money she told him crossly, 'I may have white hair, but I still have all my wits! Where's the rest?' and repeated the amount he owed her while the boy, red-faced, fumbled with a handful of change.

She gave Gina and Roz a friendly look; they had already become faces she recognised. 'What will it be today, darlings? Try my minestrone, I made it myself so I know it's good.' When they said they just wanted sandwiches, she threw up her hands and darted off to fill their order. 'No imagination!' she told them, handing

106

over the food in brown paper bags saying, 'Recycled paper!'

'Oh,' they said, startled. 'Thank you.'

They walked across the open square of the plaza, through the exit to the riverbank, on Ratcliff Walk, and sat on a bench in the newly planted embankment gardens from where they could watch the Thames.

'Did you know,' Gina said, biting into her egg salad sandwich, 'that in the eighteenth and nineteenth centuries there was a street running parallel with the Thames, called the Ratcliff Highway? It was full of prostitutes and their pimps, waiting for sailors, and thieves who got sailors drunk and stole their money, or even killed them.'

'Where did you hear about that?' asked Roz, staring at the peaceful scene in front of them; the blue spring sky, yellow daffodils and bright orange tulips in the gardens, barges slowly chugging past, tarpaulin hiding whatever they carried, a police launch speeding along with a great wake behind it, a few battered old freighters bobbing at anchor.

'I read about it once,' said Gina, throwing the rest of her sandwiches to some gulls which came screaming down to take them.

Roz said, 'I suppose in those days, there were always dozens of ships docking in the port of London, and thousands of sailors coming ashore with pockets full of money!'

'And plenty of vultures waiting for them,' Gina said with a touch of bitterness. 'The Nick Caspians of this century had ancestors!'

Roz gave her an amused look. 'You know, you're becoming quite waspish. And you used to be such a good little girl!'

Gina smiled briefly, then her face relapsed into its usual look of weary sadness, and Roz frowned, watching her.

'You're so pale! Seriously, Gina, you really need——'

'I know! A holiday!' exploded Gina. 'So I keep being told. I wish people would mind their own business!'

'OK, calm down,' soothed Roz, startled. 'Gina, it isn't like you to blow up over friendly advice!'

Gina stared fixedly at the sunlit river, the rows of buildings on the opposite bank, the distant vistas of the city of London, the spires and office blocks, the domes and towers which made the view so spectacular, and saw them all as through a dark filter, through her own misery. 'I know,' she said flatly. She couldn't tell anyone how unhappy she was, even Roz, her oldest friend. She had never been this unhappy before; her grief and pain pervaded everything in her life.

'I would go away for the weekend, if I could only make up my mind where to go,' she conceded. 'I don't have any relatives to visit, it's early in the year to go to the seaside, the season won't have started—which only leaves the country and I can't think where...'

Roz was looking thoughtful. 'How about Paris?'

Gina looked at her in surprise. 'Paris? Just for the weekend?'

'Don't sound so shocked. If we leave on Friday...'

'We?'

'I think you need company, don't you?'

'Are you serious?' Gina said uncertainly. 'It would make it much more fun for me, to have someone with me, but I don't want you to feel obliged to...'

'I love Paris,' Roz said lightly. 'And you need a guide. Paris will blow your mind if you don't have someone to take you around, and, anyway, I have my own reasons for wanting to pop over to Paris. There are a few things I want to check out.'

'Like Nicole Augustin?' Gina suggested drily, and Roz gave her a crooked little smile.

'And other matters,' she said.

Gina had told her she couldn't keep her promise to give Roz the job of Paris correspondent, bleakly apologising. To her grateful relief Roz had not been surprised, or reproachful; in fact she had sounded as if she had expected some such development as soon as Nick Caspian returned.

Roz had then asked her who else was in the running, and Gina had told her the names on the short-list. No doubt Nick would say that she was being indiscreet, but she felt she owed Roz something. It had startled her when Roz reacted sharply to the name of Nicole Augustin, but then Roz had told her she believed the other woman to be a friend of Daniel's.

Gina had frowned. 'So he'll be on her side before we even start the interviews?'

Roz had nodded. 'But then, I'm sure he'd say that *you* are on my side before the interviews start! Which balances you both out, as members of the appointments board.'

Staring at the river, Gina thought about the unknown Nicole Augustin, wondering why Nick had put her on the short-list—or was she there as a token woman among all the men? Was it likely she would get the job? She asked Roz, 'Is she attractive?'

'Never set eyes on her, but I expect she is or Daniel wouldn't be interested.' Roz was being very offhand, but Gina had known her too long to be fooled. Behind her casual expression, something was upsetting her. Gina frowned. What could it be?

She knew Roz too well to expect any answers if she asked direct questions, so she probed tentatively, 'What else do you want to check out in Paris?'

As she expected, Roz at once said, 'It's private!' Then she gave Gina a quick look, hesitated, and said on impulse, 'Oh, well, you're practically one of the family after all these years! If I tell you, swear it won't go any further?'

'Of course,' said Gina, feeling anxious as she watched Roz's face.

'Well, you remember I couldn't get in touch with Des, to tell him about Sir George?'

Gina looked blank; she didn't actually remember anything about those first terrible days after the old man's death.

Roz saw her face, and hurriedly went on, 'Well, when I was in Montreal I stayed in his apartment, hoping to find some clue to where he was, because he never vanishes like that without letting someone know! I looked around the apartment, but there was nothing—everything seemed perfectly normal, until I found an address I didn't recognise, in Paris.'

Gina was puzzled. 'You found an address?'

Roz explained the circumstances, giving Gina a wry smile. 'I wouldn't normally pry like that, but I was worried about Des. Anyway, there was no name or telephone number with the address, so I couldn't find out who lived there. Daniel offered to get someone in Paris to check it out.' She looked at Gina ruefully. 'He was talking about Nicole Augustin, as I discovered later. I'd never heard of her then, but she's an old friend of his...'

'Friend?' queried Gina, laughing. Roz didn't.

'Or old flame!' she muttered. 'Anyway, she made some enquiries locally, asked tradesmen, and the neighbours. Daniel rang me back and told me—the apartment was paid for by my father, but a woman lived there.'

Gina's mouth opened in disbelief, but no sound came out.

'A young woman,' Roz said curtly.

'Young?' repeated Gina, shocked.

'Younger than me,' nodded Roz.

'I can't believe it,' Gina slowly said. 'Your father isn't the sugar-daddy type, he's an intellectual.'

'That's what I said,' Roz muttered. 'But Daniel laughed at me for being naïve. According to him, all men are the sugar-daddy type, if they get the chance. My father is over sixty, he has always been very fit and active and he hates to admit his age. Daniel says he's probably trying to convince himself he's still young.'

Gina thought about it, her forehead wrinkling. 'So what do you plan to do? Go and see your father?'

'Of course not! I don't want him to realise I know. After all, if he wanted me to know about his girlfriend he would have told me.'

'Yes, I suppose he would. So what are you planning to do?'

'Well, I thought we might do some sightseeing in that district, around lunchtime, each day we're there. If I know Des, he'll eat somewhere nearby. He never goes far from where he's living; just to the nearest good bar or bistro. If I am with you, and have a really good excuse for being in Paris, and we casually bump into him, I need never tell him I know about the girl, and he will be free to tell me or not, as he chooses, but I'll be able to make sure he's safe and well. That's really all I want to know—that Des is OK, not ill or in trouble.'

Gina gave her a warm, affectionate smile. 'OK, so we leave on Friday?'

Roz nodded. 'There's a mid-morning plane, we'll take that, and we'll come back on Monday, if that suits you?'

They walked back towards the complex and dropped the debris from their picnic in the large litter-bins provided in the plaza. A group of men came out of Pierre's as they passed it, politely nodding to Gina and saying, 'Good afternoon, Mrs Tyrrell.' She smiled at them and answered, recognising them all as financial journalists from the business section of the paper.

As they all trooped into the lift, Valerie Knight joined them, looking very elegant in a knitted black wool suit trimmed with gold buttons which gave it something of a military air.

'Been lunching at Pierre's?' Roz asked her as the lift moved upwards.

Valerie nodded, her stunningly violet-blue eyes sliding past them at the group of men in the lift. 'Yes, with Esteban Sebastian.'

'Who?' Roz looked blank, but Gina's eyes had widened.

'Isn't it a gorgeous name?' Valerie said dreamily. 'It rhymes...Estaban Sebastian...I love it. He's one of the Caspian International executives who flew here with Nick Caspian, from Rome. He's head of marketing on the Madrid paper. I've been telling him he ought to transfer to London, and I'm giving him a quick tour of London nightlife tonight, starting with the clubs.'

Gib Collingwood, who was among the business journalists, leaned forward suddenly and said with a cynical smile, 'But will he be bringing his wife and kids to London, if he comes?'

'He isn't married, Gib!' Valerie retorted with a triumphant air.

Gib laughed shortly. 'Well, he would tell you that, wouldn't he?'

'He's only been here a couple of days,' Gina said. 'How did you meet him so soon? He must be a fast worker.'

'Well, somebody is!' Gib Collingwood drawled, and Valerie gave him a smouldering look.

The lift stopped at the open-plan editorial floor and the doors slid open. Everyone but Gina walked out. She said quickly to Roz, 'I'll book our flights for Friday, then?'

Valerie looked interested. 'Where are you going, you two?'

'Paris,' they said together, and grinned.

'Paris in the spring...can I come?'

'What, and leave Esteban?' mocked Gib Collingwood.

Valerie gave him a glance through her lashes and smiled sweetly. 'No, maybe not. I wouldn't want him to get away. Another time, guys.'

'Roz, what about a hotel? Any suggestions?' Gina asked Roz.

'Leave that to me,' Roz said. 'Expensive, or cheap?'

'Comfortable, but not grand,' Gina said as the lift doors closed. She was back early, and was wary of entering her office, knowing Hazel would still be out to lunch; she had gone to the West End to do some shopping. Gina was afraid of finding Nick waiting for her. She felt too tired to face another confrontation with him.

As Roz walked to her desk, Daniel appeared like a jack-in-the-box, his face dark with anger. 'You're late again! You're allowed one hour for lunch, not two! Where have you been? And don't give me some lame excuse about getting caught in traffic!'

'I wasn't going to,' she snapped. 'I had a sandwich lunch in the river gardens with Gina Tyrrell.'

His face was grim. 'Don't expect to impress me with Mrs Tyrrell's name. Eating with her doesn't give you the right to come back an hour late!'

'I'm only ten minutes late!'

'You're late!' he stormed. 'In future you'll get back to your desk on time.'

'For what?' Roz picked up the sheaf of cuttings from foreign papers which she had been handed that morning, and told to translate for future use. 'This garbage? I didn't become a reporter to spend all my time at a desk, translating other people's work. You never send me out on a job. If there's a foreign trip I'm the last in line for it, aren't I?'

Daniel's eyes flashed. 'Naturally!' he snapped. 'You're the newest member of the team. And the least experienced. Of course I prefer to send people who have been with us longer, and know what they're doing.'

'If I haven't had much experience yet, it's because you refuse to let me get any!'

There was a second's silence and then he gave her a cold, mocking smile. 'That depends on the sort of experience you're asking me for,' he drawled, and her skin burned.

'You've got a one-track mind!'

'Pas du tout, chérie,' he said, his voice deep and amused, and very French, then he stopped smiling and scowled. 'But now—get on with the work I gave you!'

He spun on his heel and walked away, and Roz glared after him. She ignored the grins of the other reporters within earshot. They got a lot of fun out of her constant battle with Daniel, but she wasn't giving them the satisfaction of seeing her tamely do as she was told.

Instead, she slipped off to the reference shelves running between the enormous windows. There were reference books on almost any subject here, and she knew she would certainly find up-to-date information on Paris hotels.

She ran a finger along the books until she found the volume she was looking for and reached it down, then stood there, skimming the pages rapidly, writing down the names and addresses of several suitable hotels, with their telephone numbers.

'Now what are you up to?' Daniel demanded, making her jump. He had come up behind her without her hearing his approach, as silent as a panther stalking in the jungle.

She closed the book and slid it back on to the shelf. 'Just looking something up.'

'What?'

She turned and met his eyes without flinching, her chin up. 'Nothing to do with work.'

'Give me that piece of paper,' Daniel said through his teeth.

She opened her blue eyes wide. 'What piece of paper?'

'The one in your hand.'

She slid her hands into the pockets of her jeans, and confronted him, a slender, boyish figure in well-washed denims, her dark hair almost bristling on her head and her face defiant.

'Does it always have to be a fight?' Daniel asked wearily, then both his hands shot out and closed round her wrists in an iron grip, at the same time yanking her hands out of her pockets. He turned them upwards and stared down at her empty palms. Roz stared back at him, the dark blue of her eyes glittering.

'OK,' he said curtly. 'Do I take it out of your pocket, or will you?'

'Touch me and I'll scream sexual harassment!'

Daniel fiercely threw her hands away, and then, before she could move his hands dived into her pockets and one of them came up with the paper she had hidden.

'Scream away!' he angrily mocked, knowing very well that she wouldn't.

He spread out the creased slip of paper and read the scribbled words, a frown incising lines into his forehead. 'Paris hotels? When do you plan to go to Paris?'

'Mind your own business!' Roz childishly snapped, knowing very well that she might as well tell a crocodile to use a toothbrush.

'You can't intend to go looking for Des!' Daniel said, his eyes probing her face. 'No. You couldn't be that stupid!'

Now that he had found out there was no point in refusing to talk about it so she said sulkily, 'Gina is going to Paris for a long weekend, and I thought I might as well go with her. She's booking the flight, I'm booking the hotel. And I wouldn't dream of going to that apartment—I don't want Des to know I checked up on him. I'm just going there for a short break, with a friend.'

'Good idea,' Daniel said in a voice she distrusted immediately, and handed her back the slip of paper. 'You're off tomorrow, aren't you? Well, at this time of year weekends are a good time to get hotel rooms. The best you've got there is the Phénix—it's an old hotel, and still doesn't have a restaurant, but it's cheap and comfortable.'

'I know,' she said furiously. 'I've stayed there.'

He gave her one of his mocking looks. 'Of course, with Des—and it isn't far from that apartment, is it?' Then he turned away, saying over his shoulder, 'Now get on with the job I told you to do! I want that copy in by five at the latest.'

She went home promptly that evening, and rang to book two rooms at the Phénix, but was told they could only offer a small suite on the top floor at the moment.

'But that has two rooms, both with a bed, and a recently modernised bathroom,' said the woman who took her booking. 'And from the windows there is a wonderful view of Paris.'

Roz hesitated. 'There is a lift?'

'Certainly,' she was assured.

'Then I'll take the suite,' Roz said, booking with a credit card to make certain the hotel would not give the suite to anyone else before they arrived.

The next day she and Gina took a taxi to Heathrow in good time, but were trapped in traffic on the motorway, and arrived so late that they caught their flight to Paris by the skin of their teeth. Breathlessly, they settled into their seats.

'I never thought we'd make it!' Gina said as the plane taxied into position for a take-off.

Roz was staring disbelievingly at a head some rows in front of them. It couldn't be. She was imagining things.

'Where shall we have dinner tonight?' asked Gina with almost childish excitement. 'You'll have to choose, you're the Paris expert.' She was flushed and bright-eyed. 'Roz, I'm really looking forward to this!'

The plane soared upwards and Gina gave Roz a puzzled sideways look. 'You aren't scared of flying, are you?'

Roz detached her gaze from the dark head, and looked blankly at Gina. 'Scared? Not at all, I've flown far too often to be scared. Why?'

Gina looked down at her hands, and only then did Roz realise she was gripping the arms of her seat so tightly that her knuckles had turned white. She hurriedly relaxed, groaning.

'It isn't flying that's making me so uptight!' she said. 'It's Daniel Bruneille—he's on the plane, three rows ahead.'

Looking startled, Gina flicked a quick glance to the third row in front, and gasped. 'I believe you're right.'

'I know I am,' Roz said grimly.

'What a coincidence,' said Gina.

'Coincidence my foot! He knew we were going to Paris on this flight. He knows why I want to go to Paris, too. That's why he's here. Daniel can't mind his own business, he has to interfere. I should have guessed, I did have a sort of suspicion, but I told myself I was being paranoid, imagining things.' She thought back over that conversation in the office and ground her teeth. 'He even recommended the hotel, the Phénix, said it was the best on my list. I should have known better than to follow his advice. What's that old proverb about bewaring the Greeks when they come bearing gifts?'

'He isn't Greek, he's French,' Gina protested.

'You still have to beware when he offers you anything for free,' said Roz darkly. 'Including advice. Now he knows where to find us and he can keep tabs on us.'

'You don't think he's going to contact your father and warn him that you are in Paris?' Gina uneasily asked and Roz shrugged.

'With Daniel Bruneille, who knows? He's capable of anything—and, when you think about it, why else should he be going to Paris at the same time as us?'

Gina nodded. 'Well, put like that . . . yes . . .'

Roz watched the back of Daniel's head, brooding over his duplicity. He hadn't given her any hint of his intentions, except that sudden softening of his mood, the helpful advice, the innocent smile he wore as he walked away. Fool that she was, she hadn't worked it out, though. Oh, she had been wary—but she had not put two and two together.

'Just let him come back here,' she said to Gina angrily. 'I'll tell him exactly what I think of him.'

But Daniel did not come to talk to them. No doubt because he knew what Roz would have to say, and was cunningly avoiding her, for the moment.

The flight was short; they were landing in Paris an hour later and filing through Immigration in a long queue.

'I don't see Daniel,' Gina murmured to Roz, who had been looking out for him, too.

'He has probably gone through, already—he's fast on his feet and used to travelling. He'll have slid past this lot, like a snake. We'll find him in the baggage claim area, and he'll blithely come up and suggest we share a taxi, but if he thinks I'd even consider it he doesn't know me.'

When they got to the baggage claim area of Charles de Gaulle airport, though, there was no sign of Daniel, nor outside, around the taxi ranks.

'Maybe he does know you?' Gina said, laughing. 'And he hasn't bothered to offer to share a taxi!'

Roz was not in a laughing mood. As they drove along the busy motorway into the city she was thinking hard. 'Oh, what a fool I am,' she said suddenly, making Gina jump.

'What is it now?' asked Gina, who was watching the outer suburbs of Paris flash past and wondering how much further it was to the centre of the city.

'It should have dawned on me before,' Roz muttered. 'It's so obvious! He'll be at our hotel!'

'Your father?' said Gina, bewildered.

'No, you idiot! Daniel!' Roz stared out of the taxi, glowering.

And when they walked into the Hôtel Phénix, which was up a side-street leading out of the rue de Rivoli, the first thing they saw was Daniel Bruneille just walking into the lift and vanishing upstairs.

'What did I tell you?' asked Roz with gloomy satisfaction.

Gina was speechless.

They registered and were shown up to their suite by a charming young man who insisted on opening the shutters to show them the view.

'If you look to your right, you will see the Tuileries,' he said with pride before accepting a tip and vanishing.

'I can see some railings,' Gina uncertainly said, peering down the narrow street to where she glimpsed the traffic in the rue de Rivoli.

'Don't lean on the balcony railings!' warned Roz. 'It doesn't look too safe to me. Shall we unpack and have a bath?'

'Let's go out for a walk,' Gina said dreamily, still out on the balcony staring down at the street.

Roz gave her an amused look. 'First we unpack and at least take a shower! You'll feel much better after that. Travelling is always more tiring than you think, and you don't want to collapse halfway through dinner, do you? Then we'll walk around and find somewhere to eat— this hotel doesn't have a restaurant, remember. Unless it has closed down, there's a very good bistro just round the corner. Inexpensive, but terrific!'

Neither of them had brought much luggage, so that it only took a few minutes to unpack and put away their clothes. Roz finished first, and took her shower, and then while Gina was showering Roz began to get dressed.

There was a tap at the door as she sat in her black silk slip putting on her black stockings, and she stiffened. 'Yes?' she called.

Muffled by the heavy door, a low French voice answered. 'A bottle of champagne, with the compliments of the management, *madame*!'

Roz hurriedly slid into her lace-trimmed black *peignoir* and went to the door. For a second she only saw the bottle of champagne and the glasses, on the silver tray, and stepped back to let the waiter carrying them pass her. Only then, too late to stop him entering the room, did she see his face, and realise it wasn't a waiter, it was Daniel in evening dress.

'You!' she seethed. 'What do you think you're doing, chasing us to Paris?'

'Saving you from making a fool of yourself,' said Daniel. 'What else have I done for years?' He put the tray down on a table and began to open the champagne, his thumbs slowly easing the cork out while he talked in that cool, assured, arrogant French voice. 'Where is Gina Tyrrell? I brought three glasses.'

'She's having a shower,' Roz reluctantly told him, knowing he must have deduced that for himself because he could hear, as she could, the shower running noisily in the bathroom. Gina would not be able to hear them above the sound of the water.

The champagne cork popped and Daniel expertly poured the frothing wine into two of the glasses. He turned, a glass in each hand, and offered one to Roz.

'No, thanks,' she said childishly.

'Don't look a gift horse in the mouth,' Daniel teased, charm gleaming in his dark eyes. 'Or a gift glass of champagne, either!'

The trouble was, thought Roz, her own common sense defeated her. She took the glass and Daniel's hard mouth curled in a little smile of triumph.

Then his face changed as he looked her over, her pale skin showing like pearl through the transparent black *peignoir* which covered but did not hide her small, slight body in the short black slip over a black basque with suspenders and black stockings.

'Very sexy,' Daniel said huskily and Roz blushed, her pulses going much too fast. Disturbed by her own reactions, not to mention Daniel's wandering gaze, she backed instinctively across the room.

'Gina might come out...' she muttered.

'You should always look like that,' he whispered.

She tried to make a joke of it, nervously laughing. 'It might cause a problem in the office!'

'I'm sure it would!' he said as she took another couple of steps backward, following her, his face worryingly intent. 'I would never get any work done; I'd never be able to take my eyes off you.'

Her throat closed up; she swallowed. It was an effort to say anything, and her voice sounded very odd. 'Don't! If Gina comes out...'

'She's still under the shower, I can hear the water running.' He reached out to catch hold of the wide, trailing ribbons of her *peignoir*, as if to undo it and make the robe fly open, and Roz jumped away, out through the open french windows, on to the balcony.

'Stop running away, Roz!' Daniel whispered, looking at her with dark eyes which glittered with passion, making her feel dizzy.

She was still holding her glass of champagne; she hurriedly lifted it to her lips, and sipped, in the hope of keeping him at bay.

'Delicious,' she muttered, a faint breeze fluttering the soft folds of her *peignoir*, and Daniel moved even closer, smiling crookedly.

'Do you realise that out here I can see right through that thing?'

Her face hot, she said, 'Then don't look—and drink your champagne! You were the one who brought it up here.'

'I didn't expect to find you looking like that!' he said, and she looked down blindly, trembling.

The next second, Daniel's arm slid round her waist. He was standing so close now that their bodies touched and Roz almost closed her eyes, but at that instant she found herself staring straight down into her father's astounded face.

Roz gave a gasp, stiffening. 'Des! Daniel, there's Des...'

'What? Have you started seeing things now?' he frowned, but after a penetrating look at her face, he turned to look down at the half a dozen tables laid out on the pavement opposite, outside a small bistro. Des was no longer looking up, he was on his feet now, paying the waiter, and obviously just about to leave.

'My God, it is Des,' Daniel muttered.

Roz wasn't looking at her father any more; she was staring incredulously at his companion—even from up here it was clear how young she was, a girl barely out of adolescence, tiny, slightly built, with long smooth pale brown hair and a shy, delicate face. She wore a tight-waisted, flowing lavender dress and white shoes, which made her look like a schoolgirl.

Any idea Roz had had of the sort of woman who would let herself be kept by a man old enough to be her grandfather vanished. There was nothing hard-boiled or cheap about this girl. She certainly wasn't the sexy type, either, although she had a subtle beauty in her face.

Des was no longer looking up, although Roz knew for certain that he had seen her and Daniel, and knew that they had seen him and his companion. He and the girl began to walk away, towards the rue de Rivoli, and as they did the girl caught Des's hand and held it tightly. Roz saw her father squeeze the girl's slender fingers.

It wasn't until that moment that Roz really believed it might be possible for her father to be having an affair with a girl of that age, and dismay struck her like a physical chill. 'Oh, Des, how could you?' she murmured aloud.

CHAPTER SEVEN

FLUSHED and distraught, Roz ran back into the suite, threw off her *peignoir* and hurriedly finished dressing while Daniel watched her in dark brooding.

'What are you going to do?' he asked, in French.

'Go after him,' she answered, automatically speaking French, too. 'Explain...'

'Tell him you tracked him here? You are not serious?'

She didn't look at him, her face averted, her body tense with shame and anger. 'I'm going to tell him why you and I were on that balcony just now! That it wasn't what he'll be thinking! Did you see his expression? I don't want him to go away believing that you and I are...that we...' She broke off, biting her lip. 'You know what I mean!'

'I know what you're saying,' Daniel said grimly. 'But, Roz, I sure as hell don't know what you mean! What is it to do with your father if we are sleeping together?'

'We're not!' she exploded.

'Maybe not, but how would it be Des's business if we were? What has it got to do with Des who you sleep with...or if you sleep with anyone? It is no more his business than it's your business if he is living with someone! You have a right to live your life as you see fit—and so does Des. You're an adult. So is he. Why don't you just leave it, let him go? If he wanted to speak to you, he would have waited for you to come down there.'

She knew he was right about that, and that made her angrier. 'Why don't you take your own advice—and mind your own business, Daniel?' she shouted, and that, of course, was the moment when Gina chose to emerge from the bathroom in her short black towelling robe, her hair wet and her legs bare, anxiously looking from one to the other of them.

She did not look surprised to see Daniel. Roz suspected Gina had heard and recognised his voice some time ago, and discreetly stayed in the bathroom until now.

Roz didn't bother to explain, she couldn't face Gina's worried, concerned eyes, so she made for the door and ran for the lift. Daniel could tell Gina what had happened, if he chose—Roz had a feeling he would do nothing of the kind. In his way, Daniel was as secretive as her father.

When she came out into the narrow street she turned right, as her father and his companion had done, running for the corner, where she turned right again into the rue de Rivoli, which, as usual, was crowded with shoppers. She couldn't see Des ahead, so she looked back down the elegant, formal arcades of shops, towards the place de la Concorde, then glanced across the road into the Tuileries gardens. Still no glimpse of Des. She hesitated, frowning. Should she search the surrounding streets? Would Des be planning to eat near by? Or had he gone back to his apartment?

He knew, now, that she was in Paris. She had lost the advantage of surprise. Des would be on the look-out for her in future.

Disconsolately, Roz turned back to the hotel and found Gina alone in their suite, but now fully dressed in an elegant white linen suit, a fine gold chain around her neck.

Roz paused to stare. 'You look Parisian!'

Gina laughed. 'Is that a compliment?'

'Can you ask?' said Roz with irony, then Gina gave her a serious, concerned look.

'You didn't find your father?'

Roz shook her head. 'The fox has gone to ground, I expect,' she admitted with a wry smile, looked down and huskily asked, 'What did Daniel tell you?'

'That you and he were out on the balcony when you spotted your father walking past,' Gina said, and Roz looked up to see her face innocent of any hidden meanings. If Gina had heard anything of what went on before she came out of the bathroom she wasn't going to ask questions, which was a relief to Roz.

'He said to tell you he was having dinner with a friend tonight,' Gina quietly added.

Roz stiffened, immediately convinced she knew who he would be seeing. 'Nicole Augustin!' she said with a snap, and Gina frowned.

'He didn't say. I wondered if he was going to find your father?'

'I suppose he might be,' Roz slowly said. 'But somehow I don't think so. Oh, let's forget Daniel, and everything else. We're in Paris and the night is young— let's enjoy ourselves. On Monday we've got to go back to dreary old London!'

'Do you mind? London's my favourite city,' Gina said, laughing, as they locked up their suite and headed downstairs.

'I don't think I've got a favourite city,' Roz thought aloud as they walked out into the warm spring night. 'I love wherever I am! When I was in Montreal I immediately felt at home there—of course, I was born there. But when I got back to London it felt like home, too...'

'Well, you went to school in England!' reminded Gina, and Roz nodded.

'Exactly. And now I'm in Paris, it feels like coming home, too, because I have been here so often, and some of my mother's ancestors lived in Paris. She was French-Canadian, you know; some of her family still live in France. Des once tracked them down out of curiosity—he was always interested in family trees. One branch used to live in Paris, but they moved into the country, a village near Auxerre. Do you believe in race memory, Gina? I sometimes think there's something in it.'

They were strolling along in the general direction of the Opera House, stopping now and then to look at any restaurants they passed. It was early yet, nobody would be serving dinner for an hour, at least, so they weren't in a hurry and Gina was eager to get the feel of Paris on the street, the hurried passers-by, mostly on their way home, the throb of traffic, the terrace bars and cafés, with their early evening customers drinking a first wine of the evening, or a beer, reading a paper while they relaxed after a hard day at work. Many of the shops were still open, and crowded; a florist had baskets of flowers outside, on the pavement, the air heavy with the clove scent of carnations from Provence. Office and shopworkers were diving down into the Métro, the dark green buses seemed to be crammed with passengers.

Gina's green eyes darted everywhere, trying to take in everything she could, fascinated and enchanted.

She stopped in her tracks when she saw the Opera House's ornate façade: the green bronze dome, the winged figures on each side of the roof. 'Oh!' she said, breathless, and Roz grinned.

'Stunning, isn't it? If you like your architecture elaborate!'

'Well, you couldn't ignore it, could you?' said Gina. 'I think it's out of this world. Now I know I'm in Paris. Where shall we go next?'

'To dinner?' Roz proposed hopefully, but Gina wasn't ready to stop sightseeing yet. A taxi halted near them to put down a passenger and she ran towards it, dragging Roz with her.

'Tell him where to go! Somewhere wonderful!' she said, climbing into the back.

Roz spoke to the driver and joined her.

'Where are we going?' asked Gina eagerly. 'What was that you said to him?'

The taxi shot off like a bat out of hell a second later, and Gina tumbled back into the corner of the seat. Roz gave her an amused look.

'I said Boul' Miche.'

Looking bewildered, Gina asked, 'What does that mean?'

'It's short for the Boulevard St-Michel. You'll love it. It's on the other side of the river...'

'The Left Bank?' Gina excitedly said.

'That's right, the Rive Gauche. The Boul' Miche is the heart of the Left Bank, it's for young people—full of bookshops, cafés and students, and always has been because the Sorbonne is nearby. In 1944 there was some very heavy fighting in the Place St-Michel, between the students and the German army, and a lot of students died, or were injured. Nowadays, it's a big tourist attraction, prices in the cafés can be sky high, and the food is not as good as it used to be. There were lots of family restaurants where the food was cheap but terrific, thirty years ago, Des says. You could eat peasant cooking, salt cod or *cassoulet*, but now they're often Greek or Algerian, the food isn't as good, and it's quite expensive.'

'Then why are we going there to eat?'

'We're not. We're going to walk about, have a drink, see something of the Left Bank.'

'And after that?'

'We'll eat at a restaurant I know quite well. I only hope it's still there. The trouble is, restaurants are always closing down, especially good ones which have been there for years. The patron dies and there's nobody to take over, or someone makes the patron an offer he can't refuse, or else his lease runs out and somebody outbids him.'

Gina wasn't listening any more, she was peering out of the window as the taxi drove slowly across a bridge over the Seine in a thick web of traffic. 'Oh, look, we're going over the river!'

Roz couldn't help laughing at her amazed tone. 'In Paris you drive backwards and forwards over the Seine all the time, far more than you tend to in London, where the most important buildings are all on the north side of the river. In Paris, there are big tourist sites on both sides of the river. Which reminds me, we should be able to fit in a *bateau mouche* while we're here. There's one, just below us, on the river, see the lights? You can eat dinner on it while you get a guided tour of the city.'

'How romantic!' Gina said. 'What's that over there?'

'The Louvre again, but from the other side of the river,' said Roz, and went on to point out the shapes of other buildings they began to catch sight of: the towers of Notre-Dame, the black outline of the Concièrgerie, the dome of the Panthéon.

The taxi put them down at the Place St-Michel, near the fountain, where a guitarist in a black velvet waistcoat and jacket sat playing with a tricorn hat near his feet. People passing stopped to listen, then threw coins into the hat, which the man acknowledged with a small, polite bow each time.

Roz and Gina walked on through the narrow, twisting streets of the Left Bank, past the Greek and Armenian and Algerian restaurants, emerging at last opposite Notre-Dame again. By then even Gina was tired, so they had a drink at a brasserie right opposite the cathedral before walking on along the quays, following the river for quite a way, until they reached the Brasserie Limoges, the restaurant Roz remembered from her last few visits to Paris.

The same proprietor greeted them, recognised her, too, and shook hands, saying he had had her father in the restaurant only that week, and didn't he look well? He insisted on bringing them an aperitif on the house to drink while they studied the menu.

Gina enjoyed the meal more than anything she had eaten for a long time. The atmosphere was so romantic, in the little brasserie by the Seine, watching the stars come out above them and the moon make swimming patterns on the river.

She found it hard to remember that they had only been in France for a few hours. So much had happened, there had been so many impressions to absorb, a culture shock to survive, finding herself surrounded by a sea of French speakers, she felt she had been there for days, and she yawned widely as they climbed into a taxi and headed back towards their hotel on the other side of the river.

'Tired?' Roz asked, amused, and Gina nodded, laughing. Roz watched her, thinking that Gina was already beginning to look and sound more like her old self. This change of scene, away from everything that reminded her of the way Sir George had died, of all her problems over the *Sentinel* and Nick Caspian, was what she had needed. It had given her new ideas to think

about; Paris had hit her like a strong wind blowing away
a mist from the sky.

The taxi pulled up outside the Hôtel Phénix, and Roz
paid the driver while Gina wandered in to the lobby.

Roz joined her at the reception desk a moment later,
to pick up their keys to the suite, but as they walked to
the lift Roz heard voices in the little bar which opened
out of a corner of the lobby. She stiffened, her head
quickly turning in that direction.

The lift arrived and Gina walked into it. Roz said
huskily, 'You go up, Gina, and get to bed. I shan't be
coming for a while. I've just heard my father, in the bar,
with Daniel; I'll have to go and talk to them.'

Gina looked startled, gave her a searching, concerned
look, but nodded her understanding. The lift doors
began to close and Roz walked away, fighting to look
calm and at ease but inwardly in turmoil, butterflies in
her stomach.

What was she going to say to her father? And would
he have that girl with him? Roz didn't know how she
was going to handle it, if he had.

She paused in the bar doorway and heaved a sigh of
relief—the two men were alone; Des had not brought
that girl with him. In fact, there was no one else in the
little bar, they had it all to themselves. Her father had
his back to her, but Daniel was facing the door. His
gleaming dark eyes lifted to meet hers, probing her expression like a scalpel dissecting a wound, making her
flinch and glare back defiantly. She didn't want Daniel
poking about inside her head. What made him think he
had the right to know what she was thinking or feeling?

He quietly said something to Des, who got up and
turned as Roz walked towards them.

'Hello, Des,' she said as casually as she could, and he
replied in the same tone.

'Hello, Roz, you're looking well.' Then he bent his head and lightly kissed her, twice, on each cheek, French-style.

'So are you, you look twenty years younger than your real age!' she said, with hidden irony. It was true: Des had always looked younger than his age and he still did so. His build helped: he was thin and fine-boned, not a tall man, but wiry and very fit.

He had the same colouring as herself but time had made changes in it: silvered his dark hair, paled the blue of his eyes, creased and wrinkled the once smooth skin so that now Des had a very lived-in face, lines of humour, experience and cynicism around his wide mouth and eyes. Time hadn't diminished his personality, though; he still made you feel you were with someone of enormous strength and fascination. Des had the air of someone who had done everything, seen everything, and probably knew everything, but regarded life and his fellow human beings with warmth and tolerant amusement.

He had always been attractive to women, she could remember a succession of them passing through his life over the years, but none of them had been around for long, perhaps because his roving life always broke up relationships sooner or later. Women liked a man to be there every day, not vanishing for weeks on end.

Des must be lonely, now that his wandering days were done, living alone in his Montreal apartment. Roz felt a pang of sympathy. She had not been looking at the situation through his eyes.

'Sit down, Roz,' Daniel said coolly, stretching out a hand to catch one of hers. She had meant to sit beside her father, but Daniel pulled her down beside himself. 'What will you have to drink?' he asked as the waiter came over from the bar counter. She ordered a *crème de menthe frappé*, and Des made a face.

'Sickly stuff! Have a good brandy instead.'

She shook her head.

'Well, we'll have another two brandies, waiter,' Des said, and the waiter nodded and walked back to his counter to pour the drinks.

'Been out to dinner?' Des asked, and she nodded. 'Where did you go?'

She told him and he said, 'I was there the other night.'

'I know, *le patron* told me.'

Des smiled. 'Did you eat well?'

'It was as good as ever.'

The waiter brought her tiny glass of green liqueur served stiff with crushed ice, and she sipped it while the two men watched with wrinkled noses, not yet touching their own glasses.

They were making polite conversation, like strangers, and Roz felt more and more unhappy. All her life she had been so close to her father. Suddenly he seemed to be on the other side of a high wall and she could not reach him. She looked down at her glass, pushing it around on the low bar table between her and Des.

'Daniel and I have been talking,' Des said.

She had guessed that, from their expressions when they saw her, and she had felt excluded, as she often had before, when her father and Daniel sat talking shop— but this time was different. What had they talked about tonight?

'We happened to run into each other, having dinner at the same restaurant,' Daniel said. 'As we were both with someone, we couldn't talk properly then, so we met up back here, half an hour ago.'

Daniel had been having dinner with Nicole Augustin! Jealousy struck through her like a knife wound in the chest.

Des sounded wry. 'I was somewhat surprised to see Daniel with another woman after seeing him with you not long before!'

Roz felt her cheeks begin to burn at the reminder of that scene on the balcony. 'Didn't Daniel explain that we didn't come here together?' she bit out.

'I told him,' Daniel drawled, his black eyes mocking.

'I hope you did!' she snapped.

Des said quietly, 'Daniel thinks I should tell you about Irena...'

Roz froze, noting the name, which had a musical sound, the way Des said it. The girl wasn't English, then, she thought—what was she? French? Roz began to wish she hadn't come to Paris; she was no longer sure she wanted to know anything about her father and the other girl. She almost interrupted and begged her father not to tell her—after all, why should he feel compelled to explain anything to her? It was, as Daniel had said, his life, and Roz wanted him to be happy.

'I've told Daniel about it,' Des said levelly. 'I wasn't sure what to do, whether or not to tell you. You're not a child any more, I thought you could handle it, but I wasn't sure how you would react, so I asked Daniel's advice—he knows you better than anyone else.'

She looked up, startled, and met Daniel's ironic black eyes. What had given her father that idea?

'And I advised Des to tell you everything,' Daniel said softly.

'I'd better begin at the beginning,' Des said, twirling his brandy glass and staring into it. 'Roz, when your mother died it hit me hard. I felt I couldn't stay on in Montreal, because everything there reminded me of her. So I took a job in London, on the *Sentinel*. You were barely six years old, but I'm sure you remember those first months. They were hard for you, too, and I wasn't much of a comfort to you. I have no excuses. I went to pieces. I was feeling pretty sorry for myself, I started drinking, I worked hard to stop myself thinking. I was never at home. I'd taken a flat in Hampstead, on the ground floor of a Victorian house...' He paused. 'That summer I found a university student to look after you while I was at work—you were always out in the garden, riding a tricycle I'd bought you—do you remember?'

She was bewildered—why was he talking about the past? If he was leading up to explaining why he was dating a girl of twenty, it was a rather roundabout way of getting there!

'Do you remember her?' asked Des.

'Who?' she asked, confused.

'Your nanny—she was Spanish, only twenty, taking a degree course at London University. She took the job as an *au pair* with us to support herself when the university term started again in the autumn.'

Roz groped for the memory, frowning. A face swam out of the past: golden-skinned, with dark eyes and glossy black hair.

'Grazia!' Roz fished the name out of nowhere, startled. Until that instant she had forgotten the girl existed, forgotten that entire summer, which had been wiped out by the trauma of starting school in a foreign country when she barely spoke the language.

'That's right, Grazia!' Des said. 'You do remember her!'

'Now you've reminded me, yes,' Roz said, still somewhat puzzled. 'She didn't stay long, though. I don't remember her after I started school.'

Des sighed. 'No, she left, in that September. She didn't go back to university after all; she went back to Spain, and got married shortly afterwards.' He paused. 'Grazia was Irena's mother, Roz.'

He said it so casually that Roz didn't take it in for a second. The girl he was dating was the daughter of someone who had been his daughter's nanny all those years ago! How could Des do it?

'And I'm Irena's father,' he said.

Roz felt as if she had been punched in the stomach. She went on looking at her father, her vivid blue eyes stretched to their limit, her face dead white.

Des talked hurriedly, frowning, flushed. 'I never knew anything about it, Grazia never told me. I only found out when I gave a lecture in Paris. Irena was in the audience, she was studying at the Sorbonne, and she heard I was coming so she turned up, and afterwards I sat there signing autographs and copies of my books, and I saw her watching me, and there was something so...so familiar...'

Roz felt Daniel's eyes on her profile and resented his watchful attention. She felt like screaming at him, stop watching me! Stop trying to work out what I feel, what I think! Why couldn't he leave her alone?

'Oh, I didn't recognise Irena because she looked like her mother,' Des said. 'She looked like mine, Roz! She was so like my mother, your grandmother. She had her bones, her smile, the shape of her mouth, her eyebrows!'

Roz had never seen her grandmother, but she had seen photographs of her, and now that Des had pointed it out to her she knew he wasn't wrong. There was a powerful resemblance between the girl she had seen with him and those sepia, faded photographs of a woman long dead.

She swallowed, nodding, and Des went on in a rushing, excited voice, 'She waited in the queue to get to me, and when she did she didn't ask me to sign a book, she had an old photograph in her hand, and she laid it on the table in front of me without a word. Of course, I was puzzled. I looked down at it and suddenly realised it was a photograph taken in that Hampstead garden, that summer; there was you, on your tricycle, and me, in a shirt and shorts—and Grazia. I looked up at Irena and it hit me all at once. She didn't have to tell me. I knew.'

Roz bit her lip, said uncertainly, 'Des . . . do you really believe . . . how can you be sure . . . I mean, where's the proof, after all these years? And if she was pregnant, why did Grazia go back to Spain and marry someone else?'

'She didn't know she was pregnant before she left— and she had been engaged for years,' he said. 'Roz, do you think I didn't ask myself all those questions? I'm not naïve; I've been around too long to be easily fooled. I can smell a lie, the way a fox can smell chickens. I was certain Irena wasn't lying to me. When you meet her, you'll understand why I believe her.' He looked at her uncertainly. 'Roz, is this upsetting you too much? Do you want me to stop?'

She shook her head. 'Go on, Des,' she murmured, aware of Daniel watching her sideways. He was leaning back, at ease, his long legs stretched out under the table, one arm along the back of the seat, almost touching her shoulders.

She was tempted to let herself relax into that encircling arm, but she held herself away, upright, refusing to surrender to that impulse. He would just love her to fall to pieces; it would give him a satisfaction Roz was not allowing him.

'Grazia only worked for us for three months,' Des quietly said. 'She was a shy, gentle girl, not a flirt or used to men. She had grown up in a convent. What happened was all my fault. I was very unhappy and lonely, and Grazia was impressionable. She saw me through rose-coloured spectacles, I suppose. I was a famous writer, to her, and she was sorry for me because my wife had just died and she could see how unhappy I was. She tried to comfort me and we ended up in bed.'

'She must have been in love with you,' Roz thought aloud, feeling very sorry for the girl she scarcely remembered.

Des grimaced. 'Maybe, and she was a virgin—no doubt about that. But I wasn't in love with her, I just needed what she was ready to give me, I didn't even recognise her generosity at the time. I have no excuses for myself, I never thought about that girl, or what I was doing to her. And Grazia was wise enough to realise just how things stood, so after a few weeks she went back to Spain instead of finishing her university course. That's something else I did to her. I ruined her chances of getting a better job. When she realised she was pregnant she must have been terrified. In Spain, twenty years ago, it meant ruin to an unmarried girl to get pregnant. Grazia had a very strong character; she planned to go away again, to come back to England to have the baby, but first she had to break off her engagement—so she confessed everything to the man she had been going to marry.'

Roz whistled under her breath. 'She certainly had guts!'

Des smiled bleakly, nodding. 'You can imagine how I felt when I heard all this. It was all my fault, and if I'd had any idea I would have done everything I could to help, but Grazia didn't even consider asking me. When she told her fiancé, to her amazement, he asked her to stay, he wasn't angry, although it was obvious he was hurt. He said he loved her and he wanted to go through with the marriage. He promised he would rear the child as his own.'

By now Roz was so deeply engrossed in the story that she almost forgot her father's involvement in it. 'What did she do?' she asked, even forgetting Daniel in her absorption.

Des shrugged. 'She accepted, of course; Irena says her mother was so touched by his kindness that the marriage worked out very well. He was a good man, a farmer, quiet, not much to say, not as clever as Grazia by any means, he never opened a book in his life and was out all day in his fields, but he really loved Grazia, and he was a good father to Irena. He and Grazia had two sons later, but Irena never remembers him treating her as anything but his own child. She never suspected she wasn't his child! It was a terrible shock to her, after he died, some time before I met her in Paris, when her mother told her the truth.'

Roz frowned. 'Why did she decide to tell her?'

'Irena says that Grazia felt she ought to be told because otherwise there would always be something important about herself that she didn't know. Grazia believes in heredity. Irena was always cleverer than her two half-brothers, who took after their father—they were only interested in the farm and the animals, they never read anything but a newspaper. Irena always assumed she just took after her mother, but Grazia thought she ought to know the truth, especially as Irena was about to leave Spain to go to France to do a language course at the Sorbonne. At first, Irena was appalled, and very disturbed, she told me. She quarrelled violently with her mother, and hated her for a time, she refused to believe it, but of course she wasn't sure, which was why she came to my lecture. She wanted to see from a safe distance what I was like—and slowly she began to feel she recognised me, the way I had recognised her. Nothing dramatic or obvious. But she found herself really believing it.'

Des smiled at Roz. 'And when I showed her photos of my mother she was really taken aback—she couldn't fail to see the resemblance, in spite of the different clothes and hairstyle.'

'I never felt I was much like Grandmama,' Roz said.

'You are, a little, and you're like Irena, too,' Des said. 'Or she is like you, I suppose, since you're much older.'

Roz sat very still as it sank in at last—she had a sister! A half-sister, she quickly told herself, but the excitement remained.

'Is Grazia still in Spain?' she asked, and Des nodded.

'She runs the farm now, with the help of her two sons, who both left school as soon as they legally could. There isn't much money in the family, the farm is small, so Irena was working here in Paris, to help support herself, and living in a tiny room which was very badly furnished. I talked her into moving into a flat I've rented, and I gave her a small allowance.' Des looked hard at Roz. 'And believe me, it took me weeks to persuade her to accept either! She didn't turn up to get money out of me. When you know her, you'll believe that, too.'

'Have you told her about me?' Roz asked.

Des smiled. 'Of course. She has seen lots of pictures of you and she has been dying to meet you.'

'Why on earth didn't you tell me about her months ago?'

Des looked wryly sheepish. 'I was afraid you would despise me.' He paused, sighing. 'I despise myself. I should never have gone to bed with Grazia, and then let her go back to Spain and a marriage I knew very well she didn't want any more. But I was relieved to see her go, Roz. I wasn't ready for a commitment then. I was too selfish and self-obsessed.'

'Nobody's perfect, Des,' she said gently, then asked, 'Why did you disappear from Montreal without telling anyone?'

His face changed. 'I got a phone call from one of Irena's friends here, telling me she had been injured in a car crash and was in hospital with concussion and suspected brain damage.'

'But she looked fine today!' Roz said, frowning.

Des nodded. 'She is, now. But I couldn't wait to find out how serious it was. I rang the airport and booked the first flight to Paris, and I was so worried I didn't even think of telling anyone, or making any of the usual arrangements. I just threw a few things in a bag, and went.'

'Don't tell me it was a joke!' Roz said, puzzled, but her father shook his head.

'Oh, no, it was perfectly true, but before I arrived Irena had recovered consciousness, and, as it turned out, there was no need for alarm. There was no brain damage and the concussion was mild; at first she had headaches for a few days, but she slowly recovered from them, too. She was allowed to leave hospital two days ago.'

Roz groaned. 'And I imagined all sorts of wild scenarios—from pictures of you being kidnapped to visions of you with amnesia.'

'That will teach you not to let your imagination run away with you,' said Daniel drily, and she gave him an angry stare.

'You were worried too!'

'I was puzzled,' he curtly said. 'But if you recall, I kept telling you Des was a big boy now and could go out on his own without getting lost.'

Tactfully, Des intervened. 'I'm sorry if you were worried, Roz. I should have rung to explain, but I'd no idea you had been in Montreal, or that you thought I was missing. I'll ring the Gaspards and make my apologies to them, tomorrow.'

'Good, they were very worried about you, too,' Roz said, smiling at him, paused, and then said, 'Des, am I going to meet Irena?'

He smiled back, his face relieved. 'Do you want to?'

'Of course I do! I liked what I saw of her, before I knew she was my half-sister, and now I'm dying to meet her.'

'She wants to meet you,' Des said. 'How about lunch, tomorrow? Daniel, can you join us?'

Daniel lazily met Roz's eyes. 'As I'm practically one of the family, I'd love to!'

What did he mean by that? She decided not to ask.

Next morning she and Gina spent hours exploring Paris shops—from the boutiques in the rue de Rivoli which sold top designer fashion at prices that made them gasp to the big department stores in the Boulevard Haussmann, ending at La Samaritaine, the Paris version of Selfridges, where you could buy anything you wanted under one roof.

Gina was going on to some sightseeing and a snack lunch in a café. 'I'll do the Eiffel Tower and Napoleon's tomb,' she decided happily. 'And see you back at the hotel around teatime.'

Roz had not told Gina the story Des had told her; she knew her father wouldn't want her to repeat his confidence. 'I let my imagination run riot,' she had said. 'Des isn't having an affair with the girl. She's the daughter of an old friend, and her father is dead, and Des is standing in for him, helping out with money and so on.'

Gina's face had filled with relief and pleasure. 'I'm so glad, I know how much you worship your father. You always put him on a pedestal. It was sad to think he had tumbled off it.'

As Roz drove back to the hotel to meet Daniel she thought of what Gina had said, frowning. She loved Des, but she didn't put him on a pedestal. Did she? Daniel had said something of the same kind, and she had been furious, but she knew Gina's motives were good, and that worried her.

In her suite, she put on some of the clothes she had bought that day, then went down to the bar. Des hadn't arrived yet, but Daniel was there, and his eyebrows went up as she walked into the room. He gave a whistle of surprised comment on her little black dress, sheer black stockings and delicate black high heels, on her glossy black hair a hat which was both tiny and complex, a deceptive affair of black lace veiling, a circle of black buckram, covered in black silk, with a large, perfect black silk rose.

'You look very French,' Daniel said with approval, and she gave him a derisive glance.

'The highest compliment you know! Heavens!'

He grinned. 'Sit down and stop snapping like a crocodile. Have a drink.'

She ordered a tall glass of fruit juices spiked with fizzy mineral water. She was very thirsty after walking around all morning, and she needed a drink.

'You should always look like that!' Daniel informed her.

'No, I shouldn't,' she said. 'Not in the office.'

He considered that. 'No, maybe not. It would cause chaos, judging by the way that waiter is staring at you.'

'Frenchmen always stare at women, even old, ugly women,' Roz said, ungratefully.

Daniel made a very Gallic gesture of impatience. 'Oh, have it your own way! Maddening vixen.' He drank some of his aperitif, then said offhandedly, 'By the way, Nicole suggested that you and Gina might like a quick tour of

L'International, the Caspian paper, tomorrow. She offered to take us round herself.'

Roz had to accept, and very much wanted to go, but she wished the offer had come from someone other than Nicole Augustin. With icy courtesy she said, 'I'm sure Gina would be delighted, and so would I.'

'Good, then we'll say after lunch tomorrow?'

'Yes, fine,' said Roz, and out of the corner of her eye saw Des walking into the bar with his companion of yesterday.

Daniel rose, smiling, and the newcomers joined them. 'Are we late?' Des asked and Roz shook her head, then looked quickly at the other girl.

Des said, 'Roz, this is Irena.'

'Hello,' Roz said, holding out her hand. Irena hesitated, then took it, her cold little fingers trembling in Roz's grasp.

'Hello,' the girl said in a soft, breathless voice. At close quarters she looked even younger than she had from the balcony. She looked even paler, too. She was obviously delicate.

Roz recalled the impression of beauty she had got, and was puzzled, because Irena's features were quite ordinary—a wide mouth, a small nose, high cheekbones. Her hair was long and brown, her figure so slender that it was childlike. It wasn't until Roz looked into her huge grey eyes that she knew what gave that illusion of beauty.

She's scared, poor kid, Roz thought—and suddenly leaned forward, still holding Irena's hand, and gave her the traditional family salute, three rapid, light kisses on each cheek.

Des broke into a relieved smile, sighing. Irena had lived in France long enough now to understand the significance of the kisses, and she said, *'Oh, merci, merci, Roz!'* with tears in her grey eyes.

Daniel waited a moment, then said drily, 'Shall we go and have lunch now? All this excitement has given me an appetite.'

CHAPTER EIGHT

THE following afternoon, Daniel took Gina and Roz to the glass and concrete skyscraper which housed *L'International*, the Caspian flagship in France, close to the Esplanade, in the dynamic new business centre of Paris, La Défense.

Gina stared in fascinated amazement out of the taxi window as they came in sight of the modernist architecture which dwarfed the horizon. 'Is this still Paris?'

Roz laughed. 'You might well ask! I'm not sure they've even finished building it, but I suppose you could call it the Paris of the future, God help us, like that film from the 1920s—*Metropolis*. That's what I always think of when I come here. Quite beautiful, in a chillingly inhuman way.'

'And this is where Nick Caspian has his main newspaper?' Gina said with a twisted little smile. 'How apt.'

Daniel lifted his eyebrows. 'You aren't implying that our proprietor is chillingly inhuman?'

Roz gave him a warning look. 'How much further is it to this office?'

'We're almost there,' he said as the taxi began to slow. They paid the driver and climbed out. Gina stood on the pavement staring upwards, shielding her green eyes from the dazzle of light from the hundreds of windows. There were not many people about; it was a Sunday and most offices and businesses were closed. It was a bright but chilly day, a sharp wind blew along the concrete canyons and across the open squares. A few tourists

147

stood in huddled groups listening to their guide explaining modern architecture and shivering.

'Let's go, I'm freezing,' Roz said irritably. She was not looking forward to the next few hours.

To get inside the security-conscious building was not easy, however. Daniel had to show a security pass which he had been given by Nick Caspian before he left London, and which was signed personally by Nick.

Even so, he, Gina and Roz had to provide proof of their identity and they had to wait while the receptionist on duty in the foyer contacted Nicole Augustin and she vouched for them.

A moment later, they were whisked upwards in the express lift which accelerated past the first thirty floors of the building without stopping to reach the *L'International* floor housing the editorial offices.

Nicole Augustin met them at the lift. Roz was prepared to hate her on sight—her imagination had conjured up a chic Parisian of her own age, and that was what she saw as she stepped out of the lift.

Nicole greeted Daniel first, smiling, kissing on each cheek. *'Ça va, mon cher?'*

Roz took in every detail about her: the smooth, dark hair, the eyes which had an amber tinge, leonine, faintly feline, but most of all her height. She was a good six inches taller than Roz, who felt towered over, dwarfed. Nicole's clothes were casually elegant: a purple wool tunic over smooth black ski pants which made her long legs look even longer.

Daniel introduced Gina, first. 'Mrs Tyrrell, Nicole...'

They shook hands, formally. Nicole spoke excellent English with the faintest of accents, and she treated Gina with courteous respect.

'I was so sorry to hear of the death of Sir George, Mrs Tyrrell. I never met him, but, of course, his reputation as a newspaper proprietor was very high. The *Sentinel* has a solid reputation in France, it has always been a newspaper whose voice counts, and I hope it always will be.'

'I hope so, too,' Gina said. 'I mean to fight to keep it so.'

Nicole measured her thoughtfully, and smiled again. 'You know I have been short-listed for the vacancy in Paris as the *Sentinel*'s correspondent?'

Gina nodded. 'I am on the committee which will interview you.'

Nicole made a wry little face. 'I didn't know that. I assure you, my remarks about Sir George and the *Sentinel* were not intended to flatter, or score points. I meant every word I said.'

Gina nodded again. 'Thank you.'

Clever! thought Roz cynically, and met Daniel's watchful eyes. She didn't try to hide what she was thinking from him, for once. Let him read her expression and see what she thought of his girlfriend!

'And this is Roz Amery, Nicole,' he said and the French girl swung to look down at Roz, with a cool assessment that made Roz prickle.

'Enchantée! Je suis très heureuse de vous connaître...' She had spoken English to Gina, but this time she spoke in French, quite deliberately, Roz realised. She was making it clear that she knew who Roz was, understood that she spoke French fluently, and, undoubtedly, that she was aware that Roz was a rival for this vacancy in Paris. Her voice, and what Roz saw as her faintly patronising smile, suggested that she was a superior being who didn't see Roz as any competition.

'Your father was here on Friday; he wrote a feature for us on the political scene in Montreal at the moment.

We're really very pleased with it. We may ask him to give us some more features.'

Roz's teeth met. Her father was one of the most respected men in his field—how dared Nicole Augustin talk about him in such a condescending way?

Daniel moved restlessly, and she wondered what he thought of his girlfriend's tone. 'Maybe we ought to start our tour of the paper? We don't want to take up too much of your valuable time, Nicole.'

She threw her arm around his shoulders in a comradely way, and pulled on his hair, with an intimacy that made Roz stiffen. *'D'accord, mon cher! On y va!'*

He gave her a glance through lowered lashes, smiling back, and Roz was so angry that she began to walk away from them, through the high-tech, modern offices, and behind her Nicole Augustin said in a fast, sharp French, 'Wait, please! You cannot go round alone!'

Roz waited, face smouldering, until they caught up. She ignored the look Daniel gave her.

The tour was fascinating and Nicole was a good guide, Roz had to admit that. She would happily have spent the whole day there, but she would have preferred another guide, and she knew without a doubt that Nicole Augustin disliked her as much as she did Nicole.

Like the Barbary Wharf complex, this was an ultra-modern newspaper office with state of the art technology available at all levels, and far fewer people working there than would have worked on any earlier newspapers.

Gina, as she stood by the window looking down the steep, glassy sides of the building from the thirtieth floor, had a dizzy sense of vertigo, and was glad that Barbary Wharf had not been designed as a skyscraper. The complex had a far more human feel to it than this place, and she knew that was due to the foresight and humanity of the old man she had loved so much, and still missed intolerably. It would be a very long time before she came to terms with his absence; she kept thinking he was in some other room, some other place, back in London, maybe, or at home, in his house which Gina now felt echoed with the past. She did not look forward to going back there, to be alone again.

But she returned to work on Tuesday morning feeling and looking much better. She had only been away for four days, but somehow time moved at another pace when you were in an unfamiliar place, among strangers. A day seemed to last forever, and things which had seemed of pressing importance at home rapidly faded into insignificance when you were absorbed in adjusting to new surroundings.

For a few days, she had been able to shed her problems: her grief for Sir George, her pain and anger with Nick, her uncertainties about herself and her ability to deal with the situation she found herself in. In Paris, she had felt light as air, free as a bird, and she brought some of that feeling back with her, undeclared baggage.

When Gina walked into their shared office, Hazel was opening one of the tall filing-cabinets. She looked round, one hand gripping the open drawer of the cabinet, her face lighting up as she saw her friend.

'You're back!' Then her eyes widened. 'Gina . . . that suit! You look terrific!'

'Chanel,' Gina said complacently.

'It looks as if it cost the earth, but it's worth it!'

'It did—and it is,' Gina said, grinning, and Hazel grinned back.

'Give us a twirl, then!'

Gina obeyed, turning round full circle on her toes to display the elegance of her black suit to perfection.

'That's what I call chic, and it's perfect with your hair!' Hazel said approvingly. 'Did you have a good time? You look as if you did. I'm glad to see you looking so much better.'

'We had a wonderful time,' Gina said, perching on the edge of Hazel's desk to tell her all about Paris. Hazel listened while continuing to slide folders into their allotted places, until Gina broke off with a little exclamation.

'Oh, I'm sorry, I forgot! Here I am talking about myself, and I've forgotten you had an important weekend, too. Did you get to Holland to meet Piet's parents? What happened? Did you like them?'

Hazel came back towards the desk and sat down on her chair, her hands linked in her lap. 'Well...' she said slowly, rather flushed, and hesitating before she went on. 'I liked them, and I think they liked me—you know how it is, the first time you meet someone, you try to make a good impression, but you're never quite sure. They aren't chatty, in fact they're rather quiet, but they seemed very friendly. It was Lilli I had trouble with, actually.'

'Lilli?' asked Gina, watching her friend in concern. Had something gone wrong during this important weekend trip to Amsterdam?

'Piet's sister. She and her husband, Hans, brought their two kids up from Middleburg to meet me. The kids were great: a funny, solemn little boy called Karel...'

'Carol?' repeated Gina, startled. 'That's a girl's name.'

'Not in Holland—you spell it with a "K" and it's their version of Charles. Anyway, Karel is seven, and very sweet, and his sister, Karen, is five. The funny thing was, it was Karen who looked most like Piet; she had his colouring, blonde hair, blue eyes, and the same smile. But her mother wasn't like Piet at all. Not at all! She had brown hair and brown eyes and she was very down-to-earth and...well, sort of flat...she spoke in a flat voice, she said polite, sensible things, but there was no warmth. I got the impression she didn't like me and didn't think I was good enough to marry her brother.'

'She was probably a bit jealous,' Gina quickly reassured. 'Sisters are sometimes, aren't they? I mean, they're probably proud of Piet, he must earn a lot, and he travels all over the world, works for a vast organisation—I expect his sister wouldn't think anyone was good enough for him!'

Hazel laughed wryly. 'I did get that impression.' She ran a hand deliberately through her hair and Gina watched for a few seconds before she realised what Hazel was waiting for her to see, and then her mouth dropped open and her green eyes widened.

'Hazel...a ring!' she burst out and Hazel laughed self-consciously, her flush deepening.

'Well, I did wonder when you'd notice it! I've been waving my hand around for ages in an obvious way, and I was beginning to think I'd have to push it right under your nose before you saw it!'

'I'm sorry, I never have been very observant. Let me see it, then!' Gina grabbed her hand and lifted it to display the diamond engagement ring, whistling. 'Good heavens—what a big stone!' The diamond glittered on Hazel's slim finger, a single, large stone set between elaborate gold claws. Gina knew a little about jewellery, since she had inherited the Tyrrell jewels and had learnt what she could about them. She could see at once that the ring had cost a great deal of money. Piet's family might not be too sure about his choice of wife, but Piet himself was taking his engagement very seriously indeed.

Hazel's eyes were fixed on the ring, too. 'I couldn't believe it when Piet picked this one. He didn't tell me

he meant to buy a ring, he was taking me on a tour of
Amsterdam, and we came to this jeweller's...
Bonebakker's ... funny name, isn't it? Piet said it was
the oldest in Amsterdam, and the most prestigious, and
he said very casually, "Let's go and look round". I didn't
actually think even then that he meant to buy one! Then
an assistant came up and before I knew what was happening I was trying on rings. I didn't have a clue what
to choose, they were all so lovely, but I certainly wouldn't
have dared choose this one because I knew it must be
expensive. Not that anyone mentioned prices. It was that
sort of shop. You got the feeling that if you asked what
it cost you couldn't afford it!'

Gina laughed. 'I know the sort of shop you mean!
Paris is full of them.'

'So I've heard,' Hazel said drily. 'I bet that suit cost
more than an arm and a leg!'

'You'd be right, but don't ask how much!' Gina
groaned. 'I'm trying to forget!'

Hazel laughed. 'You've never enjoyed throwing money
around, have you? Neither have I. I love buying clothes,
but I always shop around for the best price, I was brought
up to be very careful with money, so I left it to Piet to
decide which ring to buy. After all, he was paying! I had
no idea what he could afford, or even if he was serious.
I couldn't ask in front of the assistant, he looked down
his nose at me in a haughty way, as though he wasn't
really sure his shop wanted to be seen selling me anything. He looked as if he could price everything I was
wearing, and was considering having me thrown out.
When Piet picked this one I almost passed out, and the
assistant very nearly smiled, but of course he didn't because he was too well trained and showing any reaction
would have been very vulgar. He just insinuated that

Piet had very good taste and could come to the shop again whenever he liked.'

Gina giggled. 'Well, he's right, you must admit—Piet has terrific taste.'

Hazel held her hand up and gazed at it, sighing. 'I love it, Gina. Ever since Piet put it on my hand, I've been looking at it and pinching myself, I can't believe I'm really wearing it!'

'I know you're going to be very happy, you two. You make a wonderful pair,' Gina said, impulsively hugging her and giving her a kiss on the cheek.

Hazel hugged her back enthusiastically. 'Thank you, Gina.'

'Have you set a date for the wedding?'

'I haven't even talked to my family yet, but I doubt if it will be until the autumn, at the earliest, and more probably spring. We have a lot of arrangements to make first.' Hazel frowned, her face sobering. 'And a lot of decisions, too. We haven't worked out yet how we are going to manage setting up home together when Piet is always moving around and I'm based in London. Piet thinks he might leave Caspian International and move permanently to Holland, set up his own firm of architects. I could run the office side of it. But our plans are still on the drawing-board.'

'I suppose that makes sense,' Gina quietly said, hoping she was hiding her dismay at the prospect of Hazel leaving. Her private world seemed to be shattering piece by piece: she had lost the old man, and now Hazel threatened to go. She was going to miss her badly if she did leave.

Hazel gave her a quick look. 'It won't happen for ages, though,' she reassured her. 'But don't tell Nick Caspian, will you? Piet hasn't talked to him yet. About our possible move to Holland, I mean! I think Piet is rather nervous about broaching the subject.' She gave a wry grimace, then shrugged. 'Oh, well, love conquers all, as they say. I suppose it will work out in the end. In the meantime, you can talk about the engagement, as much as you like!'

'What engagement?' a voice asked from the door, and Hazel went pink as she looked round at Nick Caspian, who had just arrived, it seemed, judging by the fact that he carried a briefcase in one hand and his overcoat hung over his arm.

Gina's heart skipped violently for one beat. He wasn't looking at her, he was just focusing on Hazel, so that for a moment it was safe to look at him as much as she liked without fear of meeting his eyes. Being away from him had not broken the chain that bound her; she felt it tugging at her now, an ache that was actually physical, not just in the heart, a need that was agony to deny, although she had not weakened, or changed since the last time she saw him. Nick was ruthless and unbending in his pursuit of what he wanted, and what Nick could be, so could she. He had taught her more than he realised.

'Oh . . . I didn't hear you come in, Mr Caspian,' Hazel stammered, very pink and shy. 'I'm sorry, did you buzz for me?'

'No, I've only just arrived—do I gather you and Piet have got engaged?'

Hazel nodded, smiling, and held out her hand for him to admire her ring, which he did, seriously.

'Did you choose it? You have a good eye for a diamond. It's superbly cut, by a master, and the lustre is extraordinary. You won't forget to have it insured, will you? Or is Piet dealing with that for you?'

'I hadn't even thought . . .' Hazel said, flustered. 'But of course I will, at once, unless Piet already has!'

'He's very practical,' Nick said, smiling. 'And he knows what he's doing—you've picked a good man there.'

Hazel glowed. 'I know.'

'Well, I hope you'll both be very happy. Will you be getting married soon, or haven't you decided on a date yet?'

'Not yet, no!'

'Well, just bear in mind that I shall need to know in advance what you intend to do after you're married? Will you be going on with your job, or leaving? If I'm going to have to replace you, which I would very much regret, Hazel, I shall need time to find someone of your standard to put in your job. It isn't easy to get good staff, as I know only too well, and in this very specialised position I require an exceptional secretary.'

It was flattering and Hazel was pink with satisfaction in being told how much he valued her, but Gina had a niggling suspicion that Nick had been doing a little eavesdropping before he walked in here, and had overheard Hazel say that she and Piet planned to leave the Caspian organisation to set up on their own. It was impossible to guess how he felt about the idea of losing both Piet and Hazel, but they were both key personnel in the organisation and Nick would not want to lose them. Of the two of them, of course, Piet was the more valuable, and an old friend, into the bargain. If Nick had heard what Piet was planning it had probably been a shock.

'Yes, of course,' Hazel murmured. 'I'll give you good warning if I do decide to leave.'

Nick considered her, his dark head to one side and his eyes shrewd. 'Piet's job involves moving around all the time—as mine does! For both of us, it's an unavoidable part of our jobs, sometimes we resent it, but at the same time it's exhilarating, always seeing new places, meeting new people. We would miss it if we had to give it up.'

Gina watched him, her green eyes sharp. Oh, yes! He had been listening at the door, and this was his answer, a veiled warning to Hazel that it would be a mistake if she talked Piet into changing his job.

Hazel wasn't stupid, her eyes had a startled look; she had picked up his hidden meaning, and probably guessed that Nick had overheard her confidences to Gina.

Expression bland, he went on, 'It's a little like being married to a sailor; neither of us is ever in one place for long enough to put down roots. Not many women can put up with it.' He looked sideways at Gina suddenly, and her breath caught in her throat as their eyes met. 'People like us...Piet and myself...aren't good bets as home-makers, are we, Gina?' he sardonically asked, not hiding the personal note in his voice.

Hazel gave her a surprised, curious glance, then looked away discreetly.

Gina stared coldly back at Nick. 'No, you're not!'

'It takes a special woman to understand us,' he said, aiming the words at her like bullets.

The room seemed to throb with awareness, and Hazel hurriedly started talking again, to dispel the atmosphere. 'Well, Piet and I haven't made definite plans yet, and we don't quite know what we'll be doing, or when we'll be getting married, but it won't be for ages.'

She did not mention anything about Piet leaving the Caspian organisation and starting up on his own, and her grey eyes implored Gina not to say anything, either. Gina gave her a silent, reassuring look and Hazel smiled in relief.

'Well, don't forget to invite me to the wedding, will you?' Nick said, turning to go, then he said curtly over his shoulder, 'Mrs Tyrrell, could I have a word, please? In my office?'

Behind his back, Hazel and Gina exchanged looks. Hazel pulled a face and Gina managed to smile back, before reluctantly following Nick into his office, closing the door behind her.

Nick threw his cashmere overcoat on to a chair and dropped his briefcase beside it, turning to survey her with remote, enigmatic grey eyes, from head to foot. She had come back from Paris with more colour in her face; the shadows beneath her eyes had gone, her russet hair gleamed again, the lifelessness banished.

'Paris seems to have done you good!' Nick said.

'I needed a break,' Gina coolly agreed.

'What did you and Roz do—sightseeing?'

'Yes, we visited the usual tourist spots,' she retorted with a touch of defiance, catching a faint curl of his mouth and reading scorn into it. 'And I loved every minute of it!' she added crossly.

'Good,' Nick said absently, his eyes wandering down over her slim figure in the elegantly simple black suit. It fitted her perfectly; like a second skin, the deep lapels plunging, revealing her throat and the pale skin between her barely concealed breasts, making it obvious that she was wearing no blouse or shirt, just a bra and slip under it.

'Isn't that rather sexy for a business suit?' Nick drawled in a deep, smoky voice, and Gina looked away, a pulse beating in her throat.

'Don't you like it?'

There was a silence, then he said softly, 'Don't provoke me, Gina. Unless you're ready for the consequences.'

She swallowed and moved hurriedly, sat down in the chair facing his desk, crossing her legs and pulling her short skirt down over her knees, very conscious of Nick watching every movement.

After a brief silence, he said crisply, 'What did you think of La Défense?'

She was startled, looking up again. 'How do you know...?' But of course, Nicole Augustin must have told him!

His mouth twisted. 'I do own *L'International*!'

'Do you own Nicole Augustin, too?' she coldly asked.

'I'm kept informed of everything that happens on one of my papers,' Nick said. 'You know that.'

'Yes, I know that,' Gina said. It hadn't occurred to her that he might have been aware of their visit, but of course he must have arranged for her and Roz to visit the newspaper offices in Paris! Nicole Augustin couldn't have brought visitors in to the building without permission, and the Paris security firm which guarded the building would probably have got in touch with Nick to get a security clearance for them, and make sure they were who they claimed to be!

Nick's spy system worked even when you were on holiday! Gina felt a shiver run down her spine. Just now he had been warning Hazel against trying to talk Piet into leaving the Caspian organisation. Gina had an uneasy feeling that she, herself, would have found it difficult to get away, had she decided to do so instead of staying to fight him for possession of the *Sentinel*. Nick liked to be in control of everything around him; he made all the decisions, he seemed to her to feel he owned anyone who worked for him. How far was he prepared to go?

'La Défense was striking, of course,' she said slowly and warily. 'But I'm not sure I like modernist architecture. I felt alienated; human beings seem out of place there—as if it has been built for extra-terrestrials.'

'Don't be absurd!' he contradicted. 'If everyone had always taken that view, we'd still be living in caves and trees. You can't stand still, you have to move on, develop, grow! Modern architecture is a development of the architecture of the past; it responds to today's working conditions and its structure is based on its function...'

'I know, I've listened to Piet talking about it,' Gina said. 'I still don't like great tower blocks and vast office buildings.'

Nick's mouth hardened. 'The trouble with the British is they like to live in the past, but none of us can safely do that, Gina!'

'Double meanings, Nick?' she asked him coldly, and his grey eyes glittered.

'If you see them, then they must be there!'

'I don't live in the past, but neither am I prepared to pretend it never happened, or ignore it. The past formed the present; we have to take account of it.'

'Admittedly, but dead men don't come back, Gina. Your husband is dead, but you aren't, even though you live as though you were—walling yourself up with memories in that damn great empty barracks of a house. You say we have to take account of the past—on the contrary, I say we have to live for the future.'

'Don't try to drag James into this!' she angrily attacked. 'It was what you did that made us enemies. This has nothing to do with James.'

'Everything you ever do is involved with your dead husband!' Nick snapped. 'You turned your whole life into a monument to him! There hasn't been another man, you lived on in his family home, like a nun, you dedicated yourself to his grandfather and the family business—and, when I threatened to break through the high stone walls you had built around yourself to keep the rest of the world out, you went into panic.'

'That's all lies!' Gina furiously denied, getting to her feet. 'I'm not staying here, listening to you trying to explain away everything that's happened as my fault! You were the one who was so fanatical about winning that you tried to buy Philip's shares, to get absolute control of the *Sentinel*. No wonder you're so dead keen on cutting off the past and living in the present! That way, you never have to face up to responsibility for what you've done.'

She spun on her heels to walk out, but Nick came up behind her in one stride and grabbed her by the shoulders, twisting her round again to face him.

'Get your hands off me!' Gina broke out, trying to shove him away.

He bent towards her, his face taut, darkly flushed. 'You just listen to me! I asked Philip Slade to sell to me partly because I knew he was in urgent need of cash and was thinking of selling his shares anyway, which might have meant some problems if they had fallen into the wrong hands—and partly because you had accused me of wanting to marry you just to get hold of your shares. I stupidly imagined that if I already had an unshakeable majority of the shares you would believe I no longer needed your shares, and therefore had no ulterior motive where you were concerned.'

Gina was too angry to listen. 'You don't really expect me to believe a word you say, do you? I've realised I can never trust you, Nick, so don't try to sell me that parcel of lies. Now, let go of me, will you? It makes me sick to have you touch me!'

His face went white, then dark, angry red again. 'That's too bad, you'll just have to be sick!' he hoarsely muttered, and, without compunction, pulled her, strug-

gling, towards him, his dark head blotting out the light
for her as his mouth came down.

Gina began to shake; she could hardly stand, and her
body seemed to have turned boneless. Worse, her mind
had clouded; she couldn't even think any more, although
she tried. Her body always betrayed her, she had no
control over it once he touched her. Nick's mouth had
become the focus of her life; she felt his passion flowing
into her like a blood transfusion, desperately needed,
pouring through her veins, driving the beat of her heart.
She moaned, her eyes closed, swaying against him, her
hands clenched on his shirt, feeling his lean body's
warmth under her palms.

He lifted his head, breathing thickly, roughly and she
felt him looking down at her passion-blind face. 'Gina,
God, Gina, stop fighting me,' he whispered. 'Let's start
again.'

CHAPTER NINE

GINA felt a pain so intense that it was like a heart attack; she longed to give in and forget everything but the drive of her own desire, but Nick had betrayed her once before and she had to keep reminding herself that he might do it again. With a bitter effort, she forced her eyes open, her hands pressed against his chest, feeling the fast thud of his heart under her skin.

His mouth quivered in a half-smile, coaxing, passionate, tinged with the beginning of triumph. 'Gina...' he whispered again, and her body vibrated to the sound of his voice, but there were other voices in her head, the echo of Sir George's last few words to her, and she winced under the rush of that warning, those anguished memories.

She could not trust him. That was the bottom line. Nick was an opportunist, hard, ambitious, ruthless—he had used her before, and he would use her again, if it suited him.

'No,' she said, and saw his eyes darken angrily. The triumphant look vanished: oh, yes, he had been sure he was going to win this time and he still wasn't ready to accept that he hadn't.

'Yes,' he muttered, bending, but she twisted like an eel, out of his arms, and fled for the door, pulling it open before he could catch up with her.

Hazel turned from the filing-cabinets, a pile of documents in her hands, and Nick halted, unable to use force or coercion while Hazel watched them.

164

'I hadn't finished talking to you, Mrs Tyrrell,' he said in a terse voice, his hand clamping down on her arm.

'I have another appointment, Mr Caspian,' she lied over her shoulder without looking back at him, feeling that, like Lot's wife, if she did she might be turned into a pillar of salt.

She didn't wait for him to argue or try to persuade, she pulled free and walked across Hazel's office and out of the door, then ran for the lifts and was just in time to dive into one which was about to head downwards to the ground floor.

If Nick followed her she didn't see him, and she slackened in relief once the lift doors shut and they were moving down. She was trembling, her skin goose-pimpled with the strain of the last few minutes. How much more of this sort of pressure from him could she bear?

On the ground floor she walked unsteadily out into the marble-paved foyer, and turned towards the plaza where the sun glittered on the flying water of the new fountain. There were spring flowers grouped around it, softening the new brick and stone: yellow daffodils, creamy narcissus, golden tulips, drifts of changing colour seeming to reflect back the spring sunlight. Gina didn't really know where she was going; she paused, looked around uncertainly, then crossed to Torelli's snack bar, ordered a coffee and sat down at one of the little tables.

It took her a quarter of an hour to pull herself together, but by the time old Mrs Torelli came to remove her empty cup and wipe a damp cloth over the table Gina felt able to chat to her almost normally.

'Have a good weekend? Oh, you went away? Anywhere nice? Paris? Never been there,' the old lady said, leaning on the back of a chair. 'Myself, I always go to Italy, visit my relatives—not that I like them, I can't stand most of them, but blood's thicker than water and what do you have if you forget your family?'

'Do you all go?' Gina asked, knowing there were a number of Torelli sons, one who worked here, in the new bar, while the others seemed to be busy with their other snack bar, near London Bridge.

Mrs Torelli shrugged hugely. 'My sons used to come with me, and Tony still does, with Angela and the children, but Roberto's wife is always wanting him to go to Florida or Tenerife, or somewhere—I say to him, Berto, I say, who do you know in Florida, and where's Tenerife anyway? You have family in Tuscany, I say, uncles, aunts, cousins, you know them, they know you, and the weather is better than anything you'll get in Florida...' She grimaced at Gina. 'You ever been there? No? Don't go. Roberto says it's like taking a hot shower when you just walk down a street, the humidity is so bad. Of course, she says beaches...there are great beaches... Well, so what? Does she think we don't have beaches in Italy?'

Gina had lost the thread a little by then and just gave a weak smile. It didn't matter. Old Mrs Torelli didn't care whether she was listening or not. She was talking as much to herself as Gina.

'That's what comes of marrying a girl like Sandra. She's a bad housewife and she can't have babies. Roberto says she isn't ready to start a family, but they been married five years, and no sign yet. What do we know about her, anyway? Who is she? Where does she come from? Who knows? We never met her family, I don't think she's got one, and a girl without a family...well, what can you expect?'

She paused briefly, scowling into the plaza, and, feeling she should show some interest, Gina asked, 'Is she Italian?'

Mrs Torelli snorted, showing yellowing teeth. 'Never in this world. English. Londoner.' Her tone was disgusted, contemptuous. 'We told him! She won't fit in, we said. She isn't our sort. But he wouldn't listen. Always was stubborn, my Roberto. She can't even cook. Her pasta is like rubber. She overcooks it every time. I've seen her, stirring it in the pan as if it was soup, for twenty minutes at a time.'

'Oh, dear,' Gina said rather helplessly.

The old woman looked at her with gleaming dark curiosity. 'Your name is Gina, isn't it? Have you got Italian blood?'

Gina nodded. 'Way back; my mother was born here, but her family came from Milan. I've never been to Italy—I must go one day.'

'You'll love it,' Mrs Torelli assured her, then a new customer came in and the old woman had to go back to her counter, while Gina nerved herself to return to her office.

Nick had gone when she got back upstairs, to her enormous relief, so she was able to bury herself in the notes she had been given on the various candidates for the post of Paris correspondent, and then she re-read their own application letters and the breakdown on their previous careers.

When she had finished, she sat staring out at the spring day, her brow furrowed. She had a sinking feeling that Nicole Augustin was far and away the best qualified for the job. She was older than she had looked—just over thirty, and she had worked in Washington, London and Bonn before returning to Paris to work for the Caspian group.

Poor Roz! Gina thought bleakly. She was up against some pretty stiff opposition. It looked as if she was going to have to be patient before her career could really take off—but Roz was not going to be very happy about that prospect. She was far too ambitious. She might even decide to move elsewhere in the hope of getting what she wanted and Gina could not blame her, although she would miss Roz badly if she left London. If your path was blocked in one direction, though, it was sometimes wiser to take a new turning which might get you to your destination faster.

If it wasn't for her sense of duty towards the Tyrrell family, Gina would leave here, herself. She desperately wished she could get away from London, and from Nick. It was making her increasingly unhappy to work with him but keep him at arm's length. It would be hard enough if Nick stayed away from her, but he was ruthlessly seizing every chance he got to touch her. She should have known he would.

She had told him she would never forget what he had done to Sir George, or forgive him—she had been stupid enough to think Nick would have the decency to leave her alone after that. He might not admit it to her, but he must feel guilt over the old man's death, she had told herself. Well, she had been wrong. Nick felt no guilt and no regrets.

In fact, when she told him she wouldn't forget, or forgive, and it was all over between them, she began to think Nick had seen it as a challenge to a duel. A duel which Nick meant to win!

Suddenly she heard his voice outside in the corridor, talking to Fabien Arnaud, the editor. Gina stiffened, catching Hazel's quick glance of concern. Trying to look calm, Gina reached hurriedly for the phone and began to dial, with faintly shaking fingers.

Just as Nick opened the door and walked into the room, with Fabien on his heels, the ringing at the other end stopped and a voice said, 'Hello?'

'Philip?' Gina said, keeping her eyes on the desk. 'It's Gina...'

Philip Slade's voice warmed. 'Hello, Gina, how are you? How was your trip to Paris?'

'Wonderful,' she said, feeling Nick's eyes boring into her. 'I didn't want to come back!'

'I know the feeling. We must get together and reminisce about Paris,' Philip said, laughing. 'It's my favourite city.'

'I'd love to,' she said, tensing, as Nick strode past her desk and into his own office. Fabien followed and the door closed behind them.

Only then did Gina say quietly to Philip, 'I was ringing about the next board meeting. It will be at three and I thought you might like to have lunch first.'

'I would be delighted,' Philip said, sounding a little surprised, but obviously pleased.

'You do complicate your life!' Hazel said wryly.

Gina didn't answer; she had rung Philip on impulse, in a sort of panic at the sound of Nick's voice—but ever since she got back from Paris she had been thinking that she really must start living again instead of just existing from day to day like a refugee. Sir George had often given lunch to directors. It had seemed a good place to start, and she wanted to get to know Philip better. It was essential that they should be good friends; he was necessary to her game plan for the *Sentinel*.

She had made some other decisions, about her private life. The house was too big for her, she would definitely sell it and buy something smaller—a good flat, somewhere around Regent's Park, perhaps, or somewhere near work she thought. Of course that meant she would have to dismiss both Daphne and John. She could afford to keep them, but she simply wouldn't need them both, full time. She could easily manage with one part-time cleaner. Mostly she would be eating out, and she would drive herself to work instead of having John to drive her.

She would discuss it with them both very soon, and gently explain—they were reasonable people and they had been left legacies by Sir George. Not a fortune, but enough to make their lives easier when they retired.

At that moment the phone rang and Hazel picked it up, listened, frowning. 'Yes, I'll put you through, Signor Dionisio,' she said, and buzzed Nick. 'Mr Caspian, I have a call for you from Signor Dionisio from Rome,' she said. Gina heard Nick's voice faintly as he answered, and then Hazel switched the call through.

'Who was that?' asked Gina, and Hazel shrugged.

'Someone from the Rome offices—he's rung several times over the last couple of days. I think something is going on in Rome, some sort of flap over a lawsuit.'

Gina was reading the front page of today's *Sentinel* with raised brows. 'I'm surprised Mackay doesn't sue us over this story! It has got to be libellous.'

'Not if it's true,' said Hazel, grinning. 'And they swear it is!'

'What if it isn't?'

'Then he'll sue,' said Hazel.

'Well, let's hope it is true,' Gina said rather grimly. 'Because if it isn't it will cost the paper a fortune in damages. And even if it is true, they should have thought twice about risking publication. I know one thing—Sir George would never have used that story! His motto was: when in doubt, don't publish!'

Hazel grimaced. 'I'm afraid the Caspian papers don't operate on that gentlemanly, cautious basis. And that's why they sell more papers and make bigger profits. They publish what they think they can get away with, and quite often they do get away with it!'

Gina read the story again, frowning. 'I think I'll raise this at the board meeting. I don't feel we should publish innuendo and gossip of this type about a public figure.'

'Won't do you any good,' Hazel said drily. 'Nick Caspian has some sort of quarrel with Lew Mackay—I don't know the details, but I'm told he was very pleased with that story when it came in and he sent a couple of reporters out to see if they could dig up some more of the same kind.'

'You're kidding!' Gina said, with a distasteful look at the front page. While she was reading it again the phone rang once more, and Hazel picked it up, beginning, 'Mr Caspian's private office——' She broke off as a loud and angry voice sounded down the line, bellowing. When it paused for breath, Hazel said, 'I'll see if Mr Caspian is available, Mr Mackay. Hold the line, please.'

She held the phone for a few seconds, making a face at Gina across the room, then said into the phone in honeyed tones, 'I'm so sorry, Mr Mackay, Mr Caspian is not available at the moment; can I take a message?'

'Tell him if he won't talk to me, he can talk to my lawyers!' a furious voice shouted, then the line went dead.

Hazel hung up. 'What was that we were just saying?' she asked, laughing.

'Why didn't you tell Nick the man was on the line?' Gina asked in dismay.

'I had orders not to put him through again! He's been on the line several times this morning.'

'But obviously he means to sue!' Gina said, getting up. She walked over to knock loudly on Nick's office door.

'What?' he snarled from inside, making her jump. When he was in that mood, he frightened her, but she didn't back down; she opened the door and looked angrily at him.

'I thought you ought to know, you just had a call from Mr Mackay—he is obviously threatening to sue the paper...'

'Let him,' Nick muttered irritably, scowling. 'Was that all you wanted? Because we're busy discussing something more important than Lew Mackay, so if you don't mind...'

Gina gave him a mutinous look and would have argued but something in the level threat of his grey eyes made her change her mind. She quietly closed the door and went back to her desk, sat down and stared at nothing for a moment, then she got up again. To Hazel, she said, 'I hope Lew Mackay bleeds him white! I'm going to lunch and I don't know when I'll be back.'

'Good for you!' Hazel said, grinning.

Gina stayed out for several hours and when she got back discovered that Nick had left London again, abruptly.

'Rome,' Hazel told her. 'I knew something was brewing over there. He may be away for weeks.'

He was still away on the morning when the editorial appointments board met to choose a Paris correspondent, but, as Gina discovered to her rage and disbelief, he had pre-empted their meeting and appointed a Paris correspondent over their heads, although the appointment was such that Nick could safely pretend that it was their decision by asking them to ratify his choice.

Gina only found out when she arrived for the meeting. Fabien Arnaud waited until all the members of the board had assembled, and then made a little speech explaining that there was a late inclusion in the list of candidates.

'An exceptional candidate,' he said blandly. 'To have him as Paris correspondent of the *Sentinel* would add

such lustre to our public image that I agree with Mr
Caspian that we couldn't possibly make a better choice.'

Gina stiffened in her chair, pale with anger. After all
Nick's assurances of neutrality where editorial matters
were concerned, all his fine talk about staying in the
background, never interfering, he had coolly gone over
their heads! She looked quickly around the table to see
how everyone else was reacting, and saw her own surprise and indignation reflected in several faces, with a
notable exception. Daniel Bruneille was staring at a small
pad in front of him on which he was doodling idly, and
his face was suspiciously unsurprised. Gina's brows met.
So, Fabien was not the only one who knew what was
coming! Nick must have confided the news to Daniel,
too, and Daniel clearly approved of the new appointment or he wouldn't look so calm and collected.

Had Nick given the job to Nicole Augustin? No.
Fabien couldn't be talking about Nicole Augustin—she
was not a late inclusion in the list, and anyway, Fabien
had said 'him'. Who, then?

'Of course, Mr Caspian leaves the final decision to
us…' Fabien said at that moment, and Gina saw Daniel's
mouth twist cynically.

'But I am sure you will all agree with him when I tell
you that I am talking about Desmond Amery,' Fabien
ended with a smile which flashed around them all, in-
viting the murmur of surprise that, of course, came, in
varying degrees of pleasure and interest.

Gina couldn't suppress a gasp of shock. Des! It had
never entered her head that Roz's father might want the
job. He had been Paris correspondent to the *Sentinel* for
years until he chose to retire, and Sir George had always
been trying to tempt him back, without success—why
had he agreed to take on the job again now?

'Does his daughter know?' she asked, and Daniel's eyes lifted to look sharply at her.

'Not yet,' he said, before Fabien could answer.

In his diplomatic voice, with a soothing smile, Fabien told Gina, 'Mr Amery has not been required to attend for an interview, so he is not in London, he's in Paris now, and he decided not to inform his daughter before a decision had been reached, since she, herself, was on our list. He felt it might undermine her own interview.'

'Obviously it would!' Gina muttered. Oh, poor Roz!

'She, herself, was a late inclusion, of course,' Fabien said, and their eyes met. His were pleasant, bland, but Gina got the message and flinched from the cool brutality of it—Nick had told him that it had been at her insistence that Roz was included in the list of candidates! If Roz now got hurt, Gina could blame herself.

Detaching his eyes from her, Fabien looked at the rest of the board, still smiling. 'Mr Caspian felt we knew all we needed to know about Des Amery's career!'

Most of the others laughed, nodding. From the moment Fabien mentioned Desmond Amery their faces had cleared. It was obvious that they might dislike the idea of their new proprietor interfering in editorial appointments, but they welcomed the return of Des Amery to the staff.

Fabien talked smoothly, sliding from one phrase to another. Why hadn't he joined the diplomatic service? wondered Gina crossly. He had an ability to stick a knife into you without the smile leaving his face.

'His ability unquestioned...record stands for itself...a name to conjure with... highly respected... stands head and shoulders above everyone else on our list, I'm afraid.'

Oh, poor Roz, thought Gina again, biting her lip. How was she going to take it?

For form's sake, the appointments board went ahead as if nothing was settled, and interviewed all the candidates, promising to let them have a decision in writing very soon. Gina left the meeting in a state of agitated uncertainty—should she ignore the request made by Fabien and tell Roz before she got a letter informing her of the board's decision?

She went home to a lonely meal and spent most of the evening trying to get up the nerve to ring Roz, but decided, in the end, to sleep on it, and tell Roz face to face next day.

Roz, on the other hand, still knowing nothing of the board's decision, went to a noisy, hectic party given by a West Indian girl working as a secretary in the editorial department. Felicia lived in a small flat in a house backing on to Alexandra Palace parkland, high on the north side of London's suburban sprawl. The street was on the side of a hill, the view from her rooms was spectacular, night or day. If it was light you could see rooftops and spires for miles and miles right down to the river. If it was dark, you saw the lights of London glittering like a vast fairground.

Felicia's brother was a rock musician, his band came to the party and they played an impromptu gig, to the fury of the neighbours, who pounded on the walls, ceiling, door. There was barely room to breathe, let alone dance, but people were friendly and Roz had a great time.

She went home in the early hours, and found a message from her father on her answering machine. Des was in London, staying at a central hotel. He invited her to have lunch with him.

There were messages from Daniel, too: terse, unrevealing, becoming impatient. 'Are you ignoring my phone calls?' he demanded the third time he rang. 'I'll come round there, Roz! Ring me back, damn you!'

Had he done as he threatened? Roz wondered, crawling into bed, yawning. If so, he had had a wasted journey. Why the urgency to talk to her, anyway?

It crossed her mind that she might have got that Paris job after all, and her eyes flickered open, she stared at the ceiling, enjoying the fantasy. But only for a moment, because no sooner had she considered the possibility than she dismissed it as improbable, if not downright impossible.

She had seen her competition, waiting like herself for their interviews. She knew she had been up against talented people with far more experience than she could boast.

Maybe next time? she drowsily told herself, turning over and going to sleep in the stuffy darkness of her back-street bedroom.

She had left her answering machine switched on so that she wouldn't be disturbed if anyone rang again, and she didn't set her alarm clock. She wouldn't need to get up early, because she did not have to go to work next day. The *Sentinel* staff worked a rota which meant that you could stagger your working hours to suit yourself so long as you put in the required quota. As it was three o'clock before Roz fell asleep she didn't get up until ten next morning, then after a reviving shower she got dressed, had a cup of black coffee and an orange, and went shopping before she made her way to lunch with her father.

Over their aperitif Des broke the news to her, carefully watching the startled expression on her face. 'If I'd thought you were likely to get the job I wouldn't have applied,' he assured her, and Roz gave him a wry smile.

'I know, I weighed them all up and I could see I was being too ambitious...'

'You'll get there,' Des said firmly. 'You've impressed Fabien Arnaud, and I know Nick Caspian has a high opinion of you. One day soon you'll get your chance.'

'You diplomatically didn't mention Daniel Bruneille!' Roz said.

Her father eyed her in smiling silence and she flushed.

'He thinks I have been riding on your coat-tails!'

Des shook his head. 'You and Daniel have always misunderstood each other.'

'And always will!' she muttered, then for some reason felt very self-conscious under her father's ironic amusement and hurriedly said, 'You haven't told me yet why you're making this come-back—you aren't hard up, are you, Des?'

He laughed outright. 'Not at all. No, I was getting bored with retirement and I wanted to get back to Europe for a while—and, of course, there's Irena. She's going to be at the Sorbonne for another year, and I thought I would like to spend that year with her. I didn't think of applying for this job, though, until Nick Caspian rang me and asked if I would consider it...'

'Oh, it was his idea!' exclaimed Roz. 'I might have known it!'

Des smiled at her. 'Oh, he's a very shrewd guy. I gathered he had personal reasons for wanting to settle the Paris job with an interim appointment. He wasn't happy with any of the options open to him—in fact, I think I'm a caretaker. When I stop doing the job, Nick can put in someone much younger.' He lifted his glass in a toast to her. 'You have a year to prove yourself, Roz. Why don't you come and spend that year in Paris with me and Irena, get to know her, work with me as my assistant, get the feel of the job by actually doing it?'

She drew a startled breath, staring. 'Are you serious?'

'Very. Don't give me an answer yet. Think about it.'

She thought about it throughout the rest of the day, while she ate her lunch, talked to Des, parted from him in time for him to go in and see Fabien Arnaud at Barbary Wharf, then went home and did the housework in her shabby little flat.

She and her father hadn't talked about the nuts and bolts of the job: the pay, hours, responsibility. She knew Des would want to cover all the best stories himself: that was human nature. He had glossed over what she would do exactly, but she suspected she would be doing leg-work for him, researching the stories, making phone calls, looking up reference books. Des would write the stories, and they would carry his byline. Roz would be in the background, unknown and unrecognised. That was the negative side of the deal.

There was a positive side. She would be serving an apprenticeship. I've already served one! she resentfully told herself. But this time she would be in line to get the job of Paris correspondent when Des left. But would she? What if they gave the post to Nicole Augustin, or somebody like her?

She would be able to discover all about her new half-sister, too, of course. She mustn't forget that in her balance sheet of pros and cons. She wanted to find out more about Irena, and how could she unless they saw a lot of each other? It was obvious that Des wanted her to come, to spend time with Irena and get to know her.

They would be a family, for a year or so. Roz sighed. Well, why not, after all? It was an exciting idea.

Des had asked her to have dinner with him that evening, at Pierre's, the French restaurant in the plaza at Barbary Wharf, so she started to get ready at six o'clock. Des had told her he meant to invite several other people from the paper but as he hadn't actually invited them yet he hadn't mentioned any names, except to say he hoped Fabien Arnaud would be one of them, if he was free.

Roz had been pleased to hear that she had impressed Fabien, so she decided to impress him some more. She dressed with great care in a fabulous dark purple silk shirt and an ankle-length black velvet evening skirt, and used her favourite French perfume.

It was a warm spring evening. Days were growing longer now, and there was blossom on trees and leaves unfurling in the green London parks. The river glowed with reflected globes of colour from the Victorian lamps along the embankment as she drove in a taxi to Barbary Wharf along the fast riverside road by-passing the City of London. Roz had left herself plenty of time in case she got caught in homeward traffic leaving London, and she arrived very early at Barbary Wharf.

Feeling restless, she walked through the plaza where the air was sweet with the scent of spring flowers, and down to the river gardens where the pigeons surrounded her, begging for food she did not have.

Roz clapped her hands and they rose into the air in a clatter of wings. If only you could drive away disturbing ideas that easily, she thought. If only she could make up her mind what to do!

The sound of striding footsteps made her stiffen and turn quickly, her blue eyes alarmed.

'Why haven't you returned any of my calls?' Daniel demanded in a harsh, furious voice.

'I've been busy!' she retorted. 'What did you want, anyway? To tell me my father had got that job, I suppose? He told me himself. We had lunch today.'

Daniel's narrowed eyes probed her face, searching for clues to her reaction to the news. 'I'm sorry if you were disappointed, but I'm sure you realise we had no choice—Des was far and away the most outstanding candidate.'

'You don't have to sell my father to me. I love Des, and I know what a great foreign correspondent he is!' Roz snapped. 'But why did you put the rest of us through that embarrassing charade? We trooped through those interviews and all the time you meant to rubber-stamp Nick Caspian's decision to appoint my father. You wasted your time—you wasted ours! Why couldn't you come out and be frank? Why not just tell us that you were giving it to Des and we might as well all go home?'

'Do you think that would have made it any easier?' Daniel asked curtly. 'Not even to be interviewed? Just to be dismissed with a few words? That would have been embarrassing. And it wasn't just a charade. You all had a chance to sell yourselves, impress people—and some of you did. I'm sure that the next time a foreign posting comes up some of those candidates will be seriously considered for the job.'

'Nicole Augustin?' Roz coldly guessed, and he considered her with half-closed eyes, his mouth curling.

'It didn't do her career any harm to be in line for that job even if she didn't actually get it. Nick has decided she should be brought over to London to work on the *Sentinel* for a year.'

Roz felt a painful jab under her ribs. Nicole was coming to London, she would be working with Daniel, seeing him all the time, at work and out of it. Jealousy began eating away inside her, she was afraid he would see it any minute and turned away to walk back towards the plaza.

'So we'll be changing places!' she said over her shoulder, making her decision at that instant. If Nicole was going to London, Roz was going to Paris, where she wouldn't see them together, have to lie and pretend she didn't care.

Daniel caught her arm and pulled her round to face him, glaring. 'What did you say? What are you talking about?'

She found her mouth drying up, but swallowed and muttered, 'Des has invited me to join him in Paris for a year.'

'You aren't going!' he shouted, and the pigeons clattered up into the sky again, frightened away for a second time, their wings lit by the dying sun.

'Oh, yes, I am,' Roz said bitterly. 'If only to get away from you!'

Daniel's long fingers grabbed her arms and shook her furiously. 'You'll never get away from me, Roz. Not even if you went to the other end of the earth!'

Her breath caught and she stared up into his glittering black eyes, seeing the darkness raging in them, the emotion which burnt in their heart. She couldn't believe what she was seeing, her heart began to race so fast she felt dizzy.

'I've waited for you too long,' he whispered thickly, and then one hand lifted to touch her face, gently. 'Oh, God, Roz, I've waited for so many years.'

She was trembling, unable to speak or move. Daniel bent slowly and his mouth brushed over hers, light as air, soft as a feather, and her lips parted on a sigh.

'Stop running,' he whispered. 'Face it, Roz. I'm never going to give up. Like income tax and death, I'm inevitable, and you've been mine for years, even if you didn't want to admit it.'

Her eyes were wide and dark, her skin icy. She couldn't believe he meant it.

'You've been making fun of me for years!' she said huskily, and he groaned.

'I wanted to make love to you and you were too young, so I had to do something to keep you at arm's length!'

Her heart turned over heavily. She stared into his eyes searchingly. 'What about the other women you've dated over the years?' Her jealousy surfaced, her voice sharp. 'What about Nicole?'

He shrugged indifference, his dark face impatient. 'If any of them had meant anything I'd have married them, but I didn't, did I? I had dates, but it was never serious. I was just waiting for you to grow up and stop trying to be a carbon copy of your father!'

She remembered with a stab of misery the way he had made love to her once before, and then humiliated her. Was he playing the same game again?

'Are you just trying to stop me from joining Des in Paris?'

'I don't want you to go,' Daniel smokily admitted, his body shuddering in a long sigh.

Roz looked up at him uncertainly, aching to believe that he meant all this, seeing the drawn lines of his face, the tension in his mouth, and yet afraid to be disillusioned again.

'You always resented me! You thought I traded on the fact that I was Des's daughter.'

'I was jealous because you loved your father—and I wanted you to love me!' he roughly admitted. 'And I was afraid for you, I know what a dangerous way of life it is, being a foreign correspondent. It isn't the obvious dangers, so much; war and the threat of being kidnapped or attacked. In lots of these places you can pick up some pretty nasty diseases—however careful you are! I didn't want you taking those risks.'

'It's the life I want,' she said and saw his eyes close, felt his body shaking, a betraying tremor which ran right through him like an earthquake fault through a mountain range, giving away the turmoil hidden deep inside.

'And *you're* the life *I* want,' he muttered.

She wished she knew for certain that he really meant it. She was afraid to trust him, afraid to believe him, in case it was another game, a mockery which would leave her aching with misery again.

He opened his eyes and looked passionately at her, caught her face between his palms and looked down into it. 'Roz, if you really want the job, you must take it, I had the wanderlust for long enough, heaven knows, I realise you have to get it out of your system—but what the hell am I going to do without you? I've been so frustrated for so long. I can't bear much more of it. I love you. I need you.'

She couldn't get a word out, her face pale, her blue eyes enormous.

Daniel watched her, waiting for some response, then burst out, 'Don't you know we belong together, we always have, always will? Can't you feel it?'

Yes, she could feel it. She always had felt it, even when they were quarrelling bitterly.

'I'm never as happy as when I'm with you,' he said. 'Since you were just a kid, still at school, I've known you were for me, and I've been sure I was the man for you.'

Roz had known he was her man the first time she saw him, when she was a teenager, and now her heart melted. 'Oh, Daniel...' she whispered, and he gave a long, hoarse sigh, then his mouth came down, and she stood on tiptoe to meet it, her arms curving round his neck. The heat in his mouth made her lips take fire and she groaned, moving even closer, clasping his head with her hands, her face burning with the passion they had suppressed for so long.

'Darling...Daniel, darling...I love you...' she whispered, feverishly stroking his nape, her fingers in his dark hair.

A gull screamed overhead and startled them out of their absorption in each other. Daniel pulled his head back and looked down at her out of restless, passionate eyes.

'I've waited a long time for this...'

'Why did you wait so long? Why couldn't you tell me years ago?'

'You took a long time growing up, Roz. You were too fixated on being another Des Amery to realise that you aren't a second version of your father, you're something more important.'

'What's that?' she asked, half laughing, half serious because Daniel was being serious, almost sombre.

'You're yourself,' he said deeply, caressing the curve of her cheek. 'You're a good journalist, Roz, I think you're going to get even better, but I don't think you've ever really thought about your own talents, what you're really best at. You've just followed faithfully in Des's footsteps.'

She frowned, realising there was some truth in what he said. 'I still want a career on the foreign side, Daniel. I've built up all my skills for that.'

He nodded. 'I know, but take a hard look at yourself, Roz. Think about what I said.' He looked at her mouth, breathing hard. 'Roz...come home with me.'

Her knees went weak. 'I'm having dinner with Des!' she protested.

'So was I,' Daniel said thickly. 'He has half a dozen people coming—he won't miss us. We'll leave him a message with Pierre. If we're quick, we'll have gone before anyone else arrives and sees us.'

But as they hurried across the plaza, hand in hand, they walked straight into Des who looked down at their linked hands and then up at their faces, his expression acute and amused.

Roz blushed. Daniel grinned at Des. 'Sorry, Des—we won't be able to come to dinner after all.'

'Never mind,' Des said, cheerfully, eyes twinkling.

'And Roz won't be coming to Paris, either, I'm afraid,' Daniel added firmly.

An hour ago Roz would have indignantly told him not to make her decisions for her, but now all she did was give her father a flushed, shy smile and say, 'I'm sorry, Des, thank you for asking me to come, and I hope I will see a lot of you and Irena while you're both just across the Channel, but I'm staying in London with Daniel.'

Daniel's eyes gleamed with a triumph that made Des laugh wryly.

'OK, Roz, run along, with my blessing, the pair of you. You've taken long enough to get together, but I always knew you would, one day.'

Nothing ever took Des Amery by surprise.

Don't miss *Too Close for Comfort*, Barbary Wharf Book Three.

Gina seems determined to keep Nick out of her life, but will she succeed? And what of the beautiful Irena—will she ever find true love? Will she let Esteban Sebastian, the *Sentinel*'s marketing director, become part of her life? Find out in *Too Close for Comfort*, Barbary Wharf Book Three, coming next month from Harlequin Presents.

HARLEQUIN ◈ PRESENTS®

BARBARY WHARF

Charlotte Lamb is one of Harlequin's best-loved and bestselling authors. Her extraordinary career, in which she has written more than one hundred books, has helped shape the face of romance fiction around the world.

Born in the East End of London, Charlotte spent her early childhood moving from relative to relative to escape the bombings of World War II. After working as a secretary in the BBC's European department, she married a political reporter who wrote for the *Times*. Charlotte recalls that it was at his suggestion that she began to write "because it was one job I could do without having to leave our five children." Charlotte and her family now live in a beautiful home on the Isle of Man. It is the perfect setting for an author who creates characters and stories that delight romance readers everywhere.

BARBARY WHARF
#1498 BESIEGED

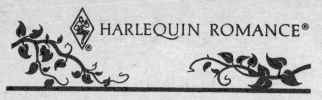

HARLEQUIN ROMANCE®

After her father's heart attack, Stephanie Bloomfield comes home to Orchard Valley, Oregon, to be with him and with her sisters.

Orchard Valley

Steffie learns that many things have changed in her absence—but not her feelings for journalist Charles Tomaselli. He was the reason she left Orchard Valley. Now, three years later, will he give her a reason to stay?

"The Orchard Valley trilogy features three delightful, spirited sisters and a trio of equally fascinating men. The stories are rich with the romance, warmth of heart and humor readers expect, and invariably receive, from Debbie Macomber."

—Linda Lael Miller

Don't miss the Orchard Valley trilogy by Debbie Macomber:

VALERIE   Harlequin Romance #3232 (November 1992)
STEPHANIE   Harlequin Romance #3239 (December 1992)
NORAH   Harlequin Romance #3244 (January 1993)

Look for the special cover flash on each book!

Available wherever Harlequin books are sold.   ORC-2

HARLEQUIN PRESENTS®

A Year Down Under

Beginning in January 1993, some of Harlequin Presents's most exciting authors will join us as we celebrate the land down under by featuring one title per month set in Australia or New Zealand.

Intense, passionate romances, these stories will take you from the heart of the Australian outback to the wilds of New Zealand, from the sprawling cattle and sheep stations to the sophistication of cities like Sydney and Auckland.

Share the adventure—and the romance— of A Year Down Under!

Don't miss our first visit in HEART OF THE OUTBACK by Emma Darcy, Harlequin Presents #1519, available in January wherever Harlequin Books are sold. YDU-G

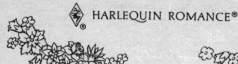

"BARBARY WHARF" SWEEPSTAKES
OFFICIAL RULES — NO PURCHASE NECESSARY

1. To enter each drawing complete the appropriate Offical Entry Form. Alternatively, you may enter any drawing by hand printing on a 3″ × 5″ card (mechanical reproductions are not acceptable) your name, address, daytime telephone number and prize for which that entry is being submitted (Wedgwood Tea Set, $1,000 Shopping Spree, Sterling Silver Candelabras, Royal Doulton China, Crabtree & Evelyn Gift Baskets or Sterling Silver Tray) and mailing it to: Barbary Wharf Sweepstakes, P.O. Box 1397, Buffalo, NY 14269-1397.

No responsibility is assumed for lost, late or misdirected mail. For eligibility all entries must be sent separately with first class postage affixed and be received by 11/23/92 for Wedgwood Tea Set (approx. value $543) or, at winner's option, $500 cash drawing; 12/22/92 for the $1,000 Shopping Spree at any retail establishment winner selects or, at winner's option, $1,000 cash drawing; 1/22/93 for Sterling Silver Candelabras (approx. value $875) or, at winner's option, $700 cash drawing, 2/22/93 for the Royal Doulton China service for 8 (approx. value $1,060) or, at winner's option, $900 cash drawing; 3/22/93 for the 12 monthly Crabtree & Evelyn Gift Baskets (approx. value $960) or, at winner's option, $750 cash drawing and, 4/22/93 for the Sterling Silver Tray (approx. value $1,200) or, at winner's option, $750 cash drawing. All winners will be selected in random drawings to be held within 7 days of each drawing eligibility deadline.

A random drawing from amongst all eligible entries received for participation in any or all drawings will be held no later than April 29, 1993 to award the Grand Prize of a 10 day trip for two (2) to London, England (approx. value $6,000) or, at winner's option, $6,000 cash. Travel option includes 10 nights accommodation at the Kensington Park Hotel, Continental breakfast daily, theater tickets for 2, plus round trip airfare and $1,000 spending money; air transportation is from commercial airport nearest winner's home; travel must be completed within 12 months of winner notification, and is subject to space and accommodation availability; travellers must sign and return a Release of Liability prior to traveling.

2. Sweepstakes offer is open only to residents of the U.S. (except Puerto Rico), and Canada who are 21 years of age or older, except employees and immediate family members of Torstar Corp., its affiliates, subsidiaries, and all agencies, entities and persons connected with the use, marketing, or conduct of this sweepstakes. All federal, state, provincial, municipal and local laws apply. Offer void wherever prohibited by law. Taxes and/or duties are the sole responsibility of the winner. Any litigation within the province of Quebec respecting the conduct and awarding of a prize may be submitted to the Régie des loteries et courses du Quebec. All prizes will be awarded; winners will be notified by mail. No substitution of prizes is permitted. Winner selection is under the supervision of D.L. Blair, Inc., an independent judging organization whose decisions are final. Chances of winning in any drawing are dependent upon the number of eligible entries received. All prizes are valued in U.S. currency.

3. Potential winners must sign and return an Affidavit of Eligibility within 30 days of notification. In the event of non-compliance within this time period, the prize may be awarded to an alternate winner. Any prize or prize notification returned as undeliverable may result in the awarding of that prize to an alternate winner. By acceptance of their prize, winners consent to the use of their names, photographs or their likenesses for purposes of advertising, trade and promotion on behalf of Torstar Corp. without further compensation to the winner unless prohibited by law. Canadian winners must correctly answer a time-limited arithmetical question in order to be awarded a prize.

4. For a list of winners (available after 5/31/93), send a separate stamped, self-addressed envelope to: Barbary Wharf Sweepstakes Winners, P.O. Box 4526, Blair, NE 68009.

This month's special prize:
A $1,000.00 Shopping Spree!

Imagine visiting your favorite department store, knowing you had $1,000.00 to spend any way you please! Perhaps you'd buy a new wardrobe...or a comfortable, elegant sofa...perhaps an oriental rug...or a large-screen TV! Well, the choice will be yours, up to $1,000.00, if you're the winner of this month's Shopping Spree!

The Grand Prize:
An English Holiday for Two!

Visit London and tour the neighborhoods where the characters in *Barbary Wharf* work and fall in love. Visit the fabulous shops, the museums, the Tower of London and Buckingham Palace...enjoy theater and fine dining. And as part of your ten-day holiday, you'll be invited to lunch with the author, Charlotte Lamb! Round-trip airfare for two, first-class hotels, and meals are all included.

BARBARY WHARF

SWEEPSTAKES

OFFICIAL

ENTRY FORM

THIS MONTH'S SPECIAL PRIZE:

A $1,000.00 Shopping Spree

NOTICE » Entry must be received by December 22, 1992.
Winner will be notified by January 4, 1993.

GRAND PRIZE:

A Vacation to England!

See prize descriptions on the back of this entry form.

Fill in your name and address below and return this
entry form with your invoice in the reply envelope provided.
Good luck!

NAME

ADDRESS

CITY   STATE/PROV.   ZIP/POSTAL CODE

(   )

DAYTIME PHONE NUMBER   (AREA CODE)

BW-M2